√35126

K
Lyon   Lyon, George Ella
        With a hammer for my
heart

                                        21.95

WITH A HAMMER FOR MY HEART

WITH A HAMMER FOR MY HEART

a novel

George Ella Lyon

A DK INK BOOK

DK PUBLISHING, INC.
NEW YORK

A DK INK BOOK

10 9 8 7 6 5 4 3 2 1

DK Publishing, Inc.

95 Madison Avenue

New York, NY 10016

Visit us on the World Wide Web at http://www.dk.com

The text of this book is set in 11 point Stempel Garamond.

Manufactured in the United States of America

Library of Congress cataloging is available on request.

ISBN 0-7894-2460-6

ACKNOWLEDGMENTS

I would like to thank the following people, whose generous support, technical advice, friendship, and/or criticism helped make this book possible—Sandy Ballard, Carol Bastian, Sallie Bingham, Louise Borden, Marie Bradby, Joy Button, Paul Cantrell, Jo Carson, Marguerite Casparian, Jan Cook, Jenny Davis, Priscilla Denby, David Fresh, Martha Gehringer, Vicky Hayes, Mary Hodges, Gladys Hoskins, Robert and Betty Hoskins, Pat Hudson, Karen Jones, Jane Wilson Joyce, the Kentucky Foundation for Women, Ann Kilkelly, Leatha Kendrick, Barbara Mabry, Jeff Daniel Marion, Lou Martin, Sue McFarlan, Gurney Norman, Ann and Frank Olson, Karen Orchard, Barbara Presnell, Marilyn Sewell, Anne and Graham Shelby, Lee Smith, Kathleen Sterling, Laura Sutton, Mary Ann Taylor-Hall, Jane Gentry Vance, Roberta White, and Dana Wildsmith.

And to Dick Jackson, my editor; Barbara Kouts, my agent; and Steve Lyon, my husband—praise and thanks for believing in this project and working with me to see it through.

Portions of this novel first appeared, in somewhat different form, in the following publications: *Ace Magazine* (Mamaw, pages 16–18, under the title "Mother Jesus"), *The American Voice* (Nancy Catherine, pages 133–139, under the title "Snake"), *Appalachian Heritage* (Lawanda, pages 5–11, under the title "Enterprise" and Garland, pages 23–25, under the title "Alone   All One"), and *Mossy Creek Reader* (Lawanda, pages 5–11, under the title "Enterprise" and, pages 39–43, under the title "Leaving").

for Dick Jackson

. . .

A summer or so after the end of the Second World War, Londoners noticed strange plants growing in the bomb craters, rare flowers flourishing. Botanists were called in and, through intense study, they made this discovery: though native to London, the plants had not grown there since 1666. The Great Fire had burned them off, buried their seed under ash and rubble. Nearly three hundred years later, the blaze and force of bombs resurrected them.

Thus, this story.

An old man lived on a hill in two buses. A bombed-out soldier, a hermit without faith. His family he'd driven off, his town he detested. He spent his time in books, booze, and dirt. And he scared away any stranger who came up his hill. Except Lawanda.

You never know who's at the door when you hear footsteps. You never know what will fall from the sky.

ONE

LAWANDA: I'm wanting to go to college. Nobody in my family has ever done it and we sure can't pay the bills, but I'm still planning to go. Last summer I tried to get a job to save money, but I soon found out there's not enough work here in Cardin for grown people, much less kids. I wasn't old enough to drive, so I couldn't work at a fast-food place. They're all on the other side of the bypass. So when we got this card in the mail in September about selling magazines, I was all excited. I had done real well selling chocolate bars door-to-door to help the band buy a tuba. Of course, I had special motivation. I wanted to *play* the tuba. But I felt even more motivated about this, so I mentioned it to my mom. She was not encouraging.

"Who do you know who has money for magazines or time to turn the pages?" School had just started and she was putting up fall beans.

"Well, nobody on this road, but girls at school carry *Glamour* around like the Bible."

"And you're aiming to contribute to that?"

"Mom, I'm aiming to save some money for college."

"I thought you was going to strap yourself to your books and win a big scholarship or something."

"I am. I mean, I'm going to try."

"And how are you going to do that knocking on doors?"

5

"I'll only do it Saturday mornings, Mom. I can't study all the time."

"There's your chores, too."

"I know."

"Well, talk to your dad."

I waited till after supper and the news that night. Dad was tired. Skinny as he is, the way he lay on the couch, his clothes could have been on a hanger.

I sat in the TV chair and told him my plan. He rubbed his eyes with his fingers and sat up.

"Do you have to furnish money up front?"

"What?"

"Do you have to pay them for sample magazines before you can start?"

"Oh, no, there's just a folder you show people. They deduct the cost of that from your first pay."

"Then it's okay by me. Fact is, it's downright enterprising, Lawanda. But you got to be careful about your territory."

"What?"

"Where you sell. They's some doors around here you knock on and you're dead."

I heard that, of course, but mostly what I heard was, Whoopee! I can do it! So about two weeks later, after my kit came in, I set out. I had on this denim jumper Mom made for me, the kind they wear now, with the low waist, and a red-striped shirt of my brother Noonie's, the newest thing he had, and he forgot it when he left for Cincinnati. You couldn't tell how big it was under the jumper. I thought how in this getup I could be pregnant and no one would know it. Like Melody Shumate. She got so sick at school, they thought she had food poisoning. What she had was a seven-pound boy.

Anyway, I also wore red jelly shoes. They're my sister Dessie's but she didn't mind. Or actually, she didn't know. She was stuck to the TV like a stamp.

I hate TV, and the first thing I sold that morning was a subscription to *TV Guide*. Old Mrs. Manning studied the folder and then studied me.

"You Howard Ingle's girl?"

"Yes, ma'am."

"Sure do feature the Smiths."

"I do look like Mamaw for a fact," I told her. "Did you see anything you wanted?"

"What? Oh, in this thing?" She waved the folder. "Do you have that TV book? Murph watches day and night. We might as well know what's on."

So I made my first sale. She had to count the money out in change from a peanut butter jar.

I had been to five houses before the Mannings' and I was getting tired. Also Dessie's jellies had blistered my little toes. My feet are bigger than hers but it's been our custom to act like they're not. With my pocketbook bulging, I sat on a rock and put my arms on my knees and my head on my arms to think. I was out Hallspoint Road. I should have said that.

I considered the girls at school I might interest in *Glamour*, *Seventeen*, or even *Cosmopolitan*. Boys who might want *Field & Stream*, *Popular Mechanics*. I began to imagine everyone I knew with a magazine in their hands and then I tried to get close enough to read the cover. Some wouldn't hold it. Others threw it at me or struck a match on their heel and set it afire. Mamaw's magazine flapped its pages and just took off. But one person, an old man, put his hands on the cover and opened it like an accordion. He began to play the most amazing tune. Not beautiful exactly, but knowing everything. I forgot about magazines, listening . . .

Suddenly, my arms slid off my knees, my forehead hit my denim lap, and I sat up. Panicked, I felt for my pocketbook and my folder. Whew! They were right by my left foot. I hadn't been asleep exactly. I don't know where I'd been. "Absent in your mind," Mom calls it, and I guess that's right.

Once I collected myself, I began to wonder who the old man could be. I only had time to try one more customer and I was sure he was it. I closed my eyes and tried to get the picture back. I couldn't, but I heard the music all right. Heard the tune anyway. The instrument was more like a harmonica. When I realized this, I listened differently and then it hit me: Mr. Garland! The old man who lives in the buses on the other side of Cade's Hill from our house. He must sit outside and play some nights or have a powerful radio, because I've heard music from up there many a time.

When I thought of him, it clicked in my mind that Dad wouldn't want me to go. "He's not bad," Dad had said when I'd asked about the man who lived up there. "Not bad, but dangerous."

"How?"

"Just any way he'd take a notion. You steer clear of him."

So I had had my warning a long time ago. Trouble was, the music was much fresher. And the image of him playing that magazine. I looked at my watch, one of my favorite possessions, all red and yellow—I ordered it from M & M's. It was 11:15. I just had time to hike up to the buses, make my sale, and be home by noon. So off I went. My toes didn't even hurt.

Mr. Garland's buses sat just below the ridge of Cade's Hill, so I came in from the back. Weeds were up above my waist. But when I came around to the front of the buses, the hillside was mowed and there was the most beautiful garden, late corn tasseling and tomatoes red as fire. I was working on courage to climb the metal steps and knock when Mr. Garland stood up between the rows.

"Well, lookee here," he said in a hoarse sort of voice. "If it ain't Miss Riding Hood come to entertain the wolf."

"Mr. Garland," I started, but my voice came out no louder than the insects in the grass. The man coming toward me was huge, with wild gray hair and a beard flowing right down to the hair on his chest. He didn't wear a shirt, and his arms and shoulders were thick and red. His cutoff khaki pants were torn and he wore no shoes.

"You catching flies?"

I snapped my mouth shut, took a deep breath, and started again. "Mr. Garland, I'm selling magazines."

"To do what? Send your eighth grade to Frankfort for a look at the floral clock?"

"I'm in high school, Mr. Garland. I'm just trying to make money for me."

I realized I was holding the folder in front of me like a shield, so I let my arm drop.

He came forward, squinting.

"Are you a Smith?"

"Well, not exactly. My mamaw is."

"Which one?"

"My mother's mother."

"I mean, which Smith?"

"Ada," I said. "My papaw's John."

"You're Howard Ingle's girl!"

"Yes."

"Didn't he tell you not to come up here?"

That got me scared, not so much of Mr. Garland as of what would happen if he told Dad.

"The truth is, I keep hearing your music at night and I thought you might like a music magazine. My dad says you read."

"Yeah," he said. "Books and minds too. Yours is pretty sharp. Come on into First Bus. This sun's a-killing me."

Now I knew I probably shouldn't go in his bus—Mom had said not even to go in people's houses—but, well, there I was. It's just like I'm going to school, I told myself.

9

First Bus was a sight.

"This is my reading bus," Mr. Garland told me. "And my company bus. Sit down right there." He gestured to the seat diagonal to the driver's. I took it and he settled in behind the wheel. I couldn't help but notice how the wheel caught his flesh right below the nipple.

"That seat you're occupying is Curtis Ballard's," he told me—Mr. Ballard's my dad's boss—"so you should feel right at home. Father Connor likes to sit here." He pointed at the seat behind his. "I told him it's because if we sit opposite each other, he thinks it's a confession booth."

A confession bus, I thought.

All the other seats were piled with books. Rows of books like in a library, rows like in his garden. And the walls, from the windows up across the ceiling, were all covered with maps.

"Where do you get the books?" I asked.

"Oh, people give them to the church, or Curtis Ballard brings them up here, or I get them from the library."

"You could be a bookmobile," I told him.

"Except I don't roll," he said. "And I'd likely shoot anyone who took my books."

That dried up my talk.

"But the bulk of my books," he went on, "come from Cincinnati. They's a place up there called the Book Hive— big outfit, five stories. I've not been there, but Curtis Ballard's told me—and I order things off of them—get a jumble box. Most of what I get don't cost over a couple of dollars, some only seventy-five cents. I get a big pile, read them, and then find a seat for each one."

"So you mean they're arranged?"

He looked at me. "I didn't think you was stupid," he said.

"And I didn't think you were mean." I sat up straight and sucked my breath in. I couldn't believe what I'd said.

10

"I don't know why not. I'm sure enough folks could have told you." Mr. Garland leaned on the wheel and the horn made a splatty sound, somewhere between a cough and a fart. I couldn't help but laugh.

"Mr. Garland," I started again, "about these magazines . . ."

"It's Garland," he said. "No mister to it. First name and last. And I might take a magazine now; you're not all that stupid. Let me see what you got."

In the end he took two, paid me in raggedy bills he slid from under a seat in Second Bus. As I started down the hill, he hollered, "Do you play guitar?"

"No," I called back. "Tuba."

"God's eyeballs!" he yelled. "Don't bring it up here!"

Threshing through the weeds, I debated whether to look at my watch and see just how much trouble I was in. I decided against it. I'd made three sales and I'd met Garland. I'd just let the good times last.

HOWARD: When I married June, I was dumb as a chair and light-headed as a willow. Any wind could blow, any hands could cart me from place to place. As long as I had June I didn't care. I figured it would all work out. Well, it has somehow. But we've had to saw off some chair legs to burn, some willow branches to mend the house with. Of course, the house gives. A house that gives ain't always a bad thing.

I guess the worst time was when I was hauling coal for that little mine at Arjay. They was shut down for safety violations after a roof fall killed Slate Jenkins and his brother. Wasn't no union there, so we all went home to starve. June and I had all five kids by then—Noonie, Ray, Lawanda, Dessie, and Jeff. Jeff was still little enough to sleep in a drawer. I was pretty scared. I looked at them—at June nursing that baby and her so scrawny, the leaders stood out in her neck; at my pockets, which didn't even have linings left to turn out. Howard Ingle, I said, what's going to save you now?

There wasn't no mine work, I knew that. I didn't own my truck, so I couldn't hire to haul something else. And I couldn't do much labor on account of my back—got busted up in a wreck when I was eighteen. Oh, I could do factory work, line work, but we didn't have any of that around here. And I sure didn't have money to move us somewhere that did.

Well, I said, other places have trucks and hire drivers. Like what? Grocery stores. I checked all them. They had what they needed. Then there was the folks further up, the ones that made the pop and milk and bread. I went to them too. Nope. They had drivers and backup drivers. What about the bus? I went to the Greyhound and the local line. Did I have experience driving a bus? No, but . . . No *buts* about it. They couldn't afford to train a man and they sure wouldn't set you in the road thinking you was driving some Ford. Okay, okay. But what?

I came out of the bus station and stared at the post office: limestone, right pretty. Then it came to me. I'd haul mail! People's love notes and doctor bills, their wish books. That tickled me. I've always liked mail, and I can't even read that good. So over I went.

Turns out you have to pass some fancy test to even have a crack at carrying the mail. If you *do* pass, they put you on a waiting list. Shoot, I said, I've got people on a waiting list at home and they're waiting for dinner.

So out I came and stood facing the bus station. A rock and a hard place. It was high noon and the heat rippled everything like a washboard—my heart included. It thumped out, What now? Now what? Now.

Then I saw a dry-cleaning truck pull up in front of a house catty-corner across the street. WE-SUIT-U, it said on the back, and there was a sign in the window: DRIVER WANTED. I bolted into the street and almost got hit.

The driver was Noll Amburgey, a fellow I'd known since we was down in the grades. He was fixing to move to Dayton, he said, because his brother told him there was big money in this construction outfit he'd signed on with.

"Who's getting your job?" I asked.

He didn't know. He'd only told Curtis Ballard he was leaving the day before.

"Look," I said, "I'm in bad need of work. Could you put in a word for me?"

"Hop in," Noll said, "and you can meet him at the end of the route."

So I did. Luckiest day of my life, next to when I met June. Mr. Ballard took me in, had Noll train me, gave me grocery money for two weeks before Noll left. "You can clean out the boiler room," he said, and I did, but it only took me two days. Rest of the time, I rode with Noll or worked patching up things at the house. I had this good deep-down feeling, like my life was taking a new turn. And it was. I been Mr. Ballard's route man for eight years; he's been my friend every one of them.

• • •

Not long after I started the job, he came in on a Monday morning and found the fire out. Building stone-cold and folks needing to work, customers coming by to pick up their clothes. And me not there to explain, much less head out on pickup and delivery.

Any other boss would have had my time card tore up before I hit the door. I was expecting something bad.

"Mr. Ballard," I said, "I know you're wondering why I didn't come in this morning, why I didn't fire the stoker last night. Lawanda, my girl who's seven, took sick yesterday morning. June tried to doctor her with what we had, and she seemed to be coming along. Then about dinnertime her breath got thick, so we put her in the truck between us— the other kids in the back—and headed over to June's mother's at Little Splinter Creek. I might have told you before—she's a healer. I don't mean bark and vinegar; I mean laying on of hands.

"You're about to say why didn't we go to a doctor, child sick like that, and go to someone close, not over Pine Mountain. Well, you're forgetting it was Sunday, hard to come by a doctor, and after food shopping the night before, hard to come by the money, too.

"Anyway, by the time we got there, Lawanda's breathing had a rattle to it. I was scared myself, and June started crying before we even got out of the truck. Mamaw just held the screen door for us, saying, 'Oh, honey. Oh, Mother Jesus.'

"She sent June to the kitchen with the other younguns. It had been raining at the top of the mountain and they needed drying off and warming up. I could hear June filling the kettle.

"Mamaw had me lay Lawanda on the biggest bed, cold in that room and not a cover on her. I went to pull up the quilt.

" 'Leave it be,' Mamaw ordered.

"And quick as a mechanic checking your points, she felt anklebones, knees, hips. Tried ribs, elbows, shoulders. I watched Lawanda's breath ease when Mamaw leaned over her, watched her face soften when Mamaw touched behind her ears.

" 'Nighthawk,' Mamaw said, her voice tight as a fiddle string. 'Sweet Mother Jesus, fly away with her pain.'

"And she reached in under the bib of her apron and pulled out a feather.

" 'Take that pain like some old dead thing to make a nest.'

"Well sir, Lawanda opened her eyes. 'Mamaw,' she said, with not even a clutch in her voice, 'where'd you get that?'

" 'Angel,' she said. 'Big old black thing. Your ma's got the kettle on. You want some tea?'

"Far as I could tell, Lawanda was flat-out cured, but by then it was raining buckets and June said we ought to stay the night. I'd of called you, but Mamaw's phone was out on account of the rain. I sure am sorry about the fire."

All Mr. Ballard said was, "Don't that beat all."

MAMAW: It was at Little Splinter Creek

Church that I saw what I saw. It's been thirty-five years and I remember that night like the nights my younguns was born.

Perry Roby had took the Spirit and was shouting "Damnation" up one side of his breath and "Praise Jesus" down the other. August, dusky dark, and the hot church keeping you mindful of the Pit. All of a sudden, a light whipped out like you'd unrolled a bolt of cloth. I couldn't see the church nor nothing in it. I couldn't hear the creek out the window. There was only this lap of light. I didn't know but to climb up into it. That light held me in its arms, it laid my head on its bosom.

And the light had a voice.

"Mother Jesus didn't do your dying," it said. "You'll still have to cross that river, like a child has to learn to sleep in the bed by itself. But of a morning, you'll wake up and I'll be waiting. I'm telling this to your hands. Don't let nobody go to bed before their time."

The light hummed something sweet as rain and it set me down in Little Splinter. My hands was so hot, my sister Gola jumped when I touched her.

"She's with us now!" I shouted, and keeled toward Carla Dixon.

16

"Praise His name!" I heard, going down, and knew they had it all wrong.

. . .

First thing I did was make a sign that said, LITTLE SPLINTER CREEK CHURCH OF THE MOTHER JESUS. Made it from boards left over from strengthening the chicken coop. I got me a poker and burnt the words in. Took me two weeks, had to wait till the kids was in bed. John said I was touched.

"More'n touched. I was knocked down," I told him.

"Your insides can knock you down," he said.

"I know that. But my insides never took me nowhere, never told me nothing."

"Yeah?" he said. "Well, your insides ain't never been this old before. You got lights going on where my ma used to have heat waves. She'd call one of us to pump water while she stuck her head under the spout. Maybe you could use a baptizing."

I didn't listen past that. No knot in the end of his string anyhow.

Next church day I went early, learned Sam Wilder was conducting the service, and told him I was aiming to testify. I had my sign under my arm, wrapped up in a quilt.

"You going to beat the Spirit into us?" he asked.

"No. I got something to show."

"More'n I've got," he said, running his hand over what was left of his hair. It was flat and yellow.

So I was called first, after "Precious Memories" and Eugene Coldiron's prayer. As soon as heads went up, Sam looked at me, thinking I would speak right where I was, but I headed up front, struggling past bellies and elbows with my sign.

"Sisters and Brothers of this church," I said, "watered by Little Splinter Creek, baptized in Redfox River, members of this Association, every one of you sons and daughters, some fathers and mothers to boot, I tell you: we have been led, but we have mistook the leading. We've seen a sign and read it clear wrong. Those words you carved on your heart about the Father, those words are lies. 'Jesus is our Brother,' you've been taught, been singing since you was a sprout. 'Father and Son and Their Breath, that good Holy Ghost.'

"Well, I been breathed on, let me tell you. I been lifted up to look Them in the eye. The heart's eye, friends, the One that sees it all. And this is what I'm here to tell you: there ain't no whiskers on Their faces. She ain't our Father. She ain't our Brother. She's our Mother Jesus and she longs to take us in Her arms."

I took the quilt off my sign and held it up.

"Mother Jesus!" I shouted as they drug me out.

LAWANDA: The second time I saw Garland was about two weeks later. Something was bothering me I didn't think I could tell my family about. And I couldn't talk to anybody at school. That's where it happened. So I thought I'd try Garland.

It was Saturday again when I hiked up there, October air so clear, sky so blue, it hurt. On the way I met two of the Messer boys in the woods.

"Squirrel hunting," Bill said.

"With slingshots?" I asked. Neither one of them had a rifle.

"We forgot the gun," Homer said. "Just heading home to get it."

Right. I could think up a better story than that.

Garland was out picking the last of his peppers that morning. There was frost predicted. He had on the same khaki shorts and an old gray shirt that barely buttoned.

"Hey there!" I called to him. "It's me, Lawanda!"

"What're you selling?" he hollered back.

"Nothing. I just want to talk."

"Well, come over here and give me a hand with the harvest."

He had bell peppers—green, red, and yellow—banana

peppers, even jalapeños. "Don't rub around your face when you pick them fellers," he warned, and handed me a cardboard box. His plants were almost bushes, sturdy, full, with big glossy leaves.

"Do you eat all these peppers yourself?" I asked, snapping my first one from the plant and dropping it in the box.

"No sir," he said. "I make shoes out of them."

I looked at him sideways. He wasn't smiling.

"Bet they give you the hotfoot."

He made a face. "What I can't use, I give to Curtis Ballard or Father Connor."

"Does the priest really come up here?" I'd thought maybe he was kidding when he said that the first time.

"Comes regular. Brings holy water for my bus radiators."

"But you said they don't run." He rolled his eyes. "Does he come just to visit? You're not Catholic, are you?"

"Naw." Garland spat, then threw a rotten pepper down the hill. "Father Connor brings me books. He aims to wean me off the bottle, keep me out of Hell."

"And Mr. Ballard?"

Garland straightened up. He stretched, arms up over his head, groaning a little. I could see his navel. This was embarrassing, which it hadn't been when he had no shirt on at all.

"Curtis brings food and what it takes for the garden. He means to keep me out of jail."

"Oh," I said. "I wondered where you got your food."

"Not out of magazines! And it's a good thing too. When am I going to get that hotshot review you sold me?"

"Four to six weeks, the form said, and it's only been two."

"Huh! A month if it was a day. Look at you. Your hair's a full foot longer."

"It is not!" The idea of a smile crossed his face. "Are we about done?"

"I reckon," he said. "Come on." He left the peppers by

the door of First Bus. I followed him in. We sat in the same places as before.

"So what hauled you up this way again—bus reclamation?"

"There's this boy at school—"

"Oh, no," Garland interrupted. "Don't hold me hostage in no boy-girl skirmish."

"It's not like that! He's just moved to Cardin from Little Splinter Creek, where Mamaw lives, and he's telling people she's a witch."

"Whoee! Ada Smith astride a broom!"

"It's not funny! Mr. Knight, my civics teacher, was talking about witch-hunts and how there's no such thing as witches, and Jimmy Minniard, who's only been there two days, says, 'They may not be real, but there's one where I came from!' Everybody laughed. Me, too. I thought he was from another county.

"Then Mr. Knight says, 'That's a serious thing to say.'

"And Jimmy says, 'I know. You should see her. Big crazy woman, goes around singing and healing people with feathers.'

"My heart about stopped."

"Is it true?" Garland asked.

"My mamaw is *not* crazy," I told him. Then I explained to him as best I could about Mother Jesus.

Garland studied the maps on the ceiling for a long time. Finally he said, "One thing's for sure, Lawanda. They ain't nothing you can do about what folks say." He slapped the steering wheel for emphasis.

"I know *that*." He disappointed me. "I just want to hear what you think about it—her having a vision and all. Do you think she really saw God?"

"God?" He hooted. He heaved himself up and lumbered down the length of the bus. Then he came forward slowly, chanting and slapping the seats:

21

"Damsels
climb hills
to talk
theology
with
crazy old men
like me—
WHOOEE!"

I couldn't help but laugh.

"But really," I insisted, "I want to know what you think."

He settled back into his seat. "I don't know about light striking Ada Smith, but I know they's plenty of darkness falling all around. And it don't heal people. I don't expect it gets thrown out of church, either. Most likely being churched is a sign in her favor. But you know your mamaw. Would she kiss the devil's hind foot?"

I shook my head.

"Ever cook horny toads? Drink blood?"

I laughed again. "No. All she did was have that vision."

"And it cost her?"

"It sure did."

We were quiet awhile. The bus door was open and I could hear crickets singing.

"Now it's costing you," Garland said.

I nodded. He stood up and waved his arms. "Sins of the mothers shall be visited . . ." But his old-time preacher voice faded.

"That's not funny, either," I told him, "but thanks for listening." I got up to go.

He bowed as I left the bus.

"The truth stinks," he said.

GARLAND: Now I live in a bus, two buses, matter of fact. One's full of books. Other one, if I don't watch out, is full of bottles. Come summer, I got the biggest garden you ever did see. My corn runs around the hill, beans climb like something Jack might have planted. I got blackberries, strawberries, fruit trees. Curtis Ballard give me the seed, the little old plants to set out. Says it'll keep me out of trouble. It won't. But when I'm not drunk, it keeps me out of the bus. And gives me a mess of things to eat. In July I had enough zucchini, I could roll them off the hill and kill my enemies.

You think I'm a mad old man. Well, I'm none too pleased and that's the truth. But I've got all my marbles. They may be fried but I've got them. Shoot them from one end of this bus to the other anytime I take a notion. Pickle them like cucumbers.

And pumpkins. Lord God, I've got enough pumpkins on the vine down there to light the streets of meanness for every child in the county. Now what's an old man supposed to do with pumpkins? Blast them to flying mush with my gun? Back over them with a truck? Never did like to carve the fool things.

Their faces is too much like devil spirits. Don't think I don't know. I done my time in Hell. It was called the service.

23

The armed forces. Let me tell you, they's more ways to die than to get your brains blowed out. Get splashed with your buddy's brains, for instance. March over what's left of men you've just killed. Step careful, the big boys say, and don't look down. That ain't easy. Once I tried to shake a piece of brush, something, loose from my boot, but it stuck right where the pants was tucked in. I poked at it with my gun. God Almighty, if it weren't a hand, thick old hand, hairy, with a ring on it.

And when I came home—we weren't living in a bus then; me and my wife had a little dwelling house up around Partridge—damned if I could set down and fall to and go back to teaching school. How could I look anybody's kids in the eye? So I tried work in the mines and then construction like her daddy offered. I wasn't lazy. In my day I was as workbrickle as the next. But after a week on the job, I couldn't go out the door. Didn't want her and the children going neither. Soon as I left, they'd come apart. That's what frightened me. By the time I set a charge in the mine, it was them I was blowing up. I'd run back yelling, "Fire!" like always, but it wasn't coal I heard splintering; it wasn't chunks of black rock I loaded. It was their hands, their little bitty feet. Knots in the wood when I worked construction—they were eyes. You think I could take a saw to that or drive it full of nails?

Got so's I wouldn't be there no time before I'd have to vomit, run home, and tell Nora to get them all in, set them down where I could see them. I counted their toes, ears, had to get the boy to take down his pants so I could see. "We're all here," Nora would say. "Garland, we're all here."

It drove them off, the war did. You can see why. Scared them, wore them out. No money to feed them anyhow. I never got that disability till I laid up drunk the summer after they left. So I'm here alone. Been that way thirty year. I quit counting my parts. What I got, I got. But I count my buses, one, two, and my friends, Father Connor and Curtis. Damned if I'm going to count them pumpkins though. Ugly sons of bitches can count theirselves.

LAWANDA: The next day was Sunday and I rode over with Mom, who had to take Mamaw a quilt top. That's one of Mamaw's jobs—she runs up quilts for people. By machine. Some folks look down their noses at that, but Mamaw says she can do it a lot cheaper and faster that way than she could by hand, and besides, her hands are shaky and her eyes clouded over. She has big fingers, too, but I don't know if that matters.

Anyway, I mentioned to Mom that I wanted to talk to Mamaw about something. She wanted to know what.

"God," I told her.

"Oh, Lawanda, don't do this to me!"

"What?"

"Don't drag out Mommy's old stories."

"Mom, it's important."

"I don't care. If I have to listen to that tale of Mother Jesus again, I'll pull my hair out."

Sheesh. I didn't know she felt like that. I didn't want to hurt her, but I did want to hear Mamaw on the subject. I watched the road, the hillside, the swoop of blazing maples.

"Look, Mom, this boy at school—he's in my civics class—says Mamaw is a witch, and everybody's bugging me, and I just want something to say."

Mom bit her lip and clutched the wheel. The rings slid

down her finger bones. More to herself than me, she said, "The very thing you want to forget about, your kids can't wait to dig up."

"But you're the one who told me in the first place," I reminded her. "Mamaw hardly ever mentions it."

"I just wanted you to be *prepared*," Mom said, her voice tired. "I didn't want kids to make fun of you and you not know why."

"But they didn't till now."

"It's a miracle."

I laughed but Mom didn't. I don't think she got it.

We kept driving. We were across the mountain now and coming down into the crooked valley. Just turn to the left at Turner's Grab 'n' Go, drive three miles up the creek, and we'd be there.

"I always thought you and Mamaw got along," I said.

"Lawanda!" Mom's cheeks got red. "Saying you get along with Mommy is like saying you get along with fire."

We hit a dip too fast and my stomach flew up to my shoulders. I studied Mom. She was wearing white "cush shoes"— that's what she calls imitation SAS sandals—stockings, a lime green wraparound skirt, a yellow-and-white-striped top, and her opal pendant. She's skinny and tough-looking, with curly blond-gray hair cut close. Her blue eyes were fierce behind brown plastic glasses, one temple of which was held on with a safety pin. Mom. Drives fast. Cooks fast. Makes beds and folds laundry like there is no tomorrow.

"Just slow down, Junie," Dad will say. "The Kingdom's not coming till Sunday week."

"Maybe not," she'll answer, "but somebody's got to see that we're in clean clothes."

Mamaw's as big and slow as Mom is small and fast. I don't mean slow in her mind; I mean careful, weighing. Mom is like a needle flashing through cloth. Mamaw reels out steady like the thread.

I was still thinking all this when we pulled into the gravel of Mamaw's drive. Papaw was sitting on the porch, chewing tobacco and watching for us.

"Lord, Junie," he said, hitching up his pants and coming down the steps, "where'd you get that big old girl?"

"Kmart," she said, reaching up to pat his bony shoulders.

"Well, come hug my neck, youngun," he called, and I did. He was hard and leathery and smelled like wood smoke as well as that Red Man he chews.

"Where's Mamaw?" I asked.

"On in the kitchen, I reckon, cleaning up from dinner. She said send you women on back."

Now push comes to shove, I thought, but Mom just said, "You go on, Lawanda. I'll sit out here with your papaw. Tell Mommy I'll bring in the quilt top when you get done."

I smiled thanks at her, then went on in, letting the screen door bang just enough to alert Mamaw. "Hello!" I called into the stillness.

"Come on back, Lawanda. I'm knee-deep in pot vessels."

Mamaw's kitchen crosses the whole back of the house, with work space at one end and a round oak table at the other. It's plain and scrubbed and always full of light.

"Want a chicken leg?" she asked as I stepped in.

"No thanks."

"How about some tea?"

"Sure." I got a glass from the drain board and went for the refrigerator.

"Where's your ma? Or did you fly over that hill?"

"She's out on the porch with Papaw. She'll be in as soon as—well, Mamaw, I want to ask you something."

She turned around from the sink, wiping her hands on her apron. "Yes?" she said.

And that one word spooked me, I can't explain why. It didn't sound like Mamaw's voice, but like someone far, far away, like a voice from a well. I didn't say anything, just stood there with my mouth open and a shiver starting at the back of my neck.

Mamaw tilted her head and looked at me, then smiled. "You get yourself settled," she said, "while I take them Smiths some tea."

In a minute she was back, seated at the table. Some of her hair had come loose from the bun and been steamed into a gray cloud around her face. Her Mother Hubbard apron was damp in front but she didn't seem to notice.

"Ask away," she said, "but if it takes too long, I may go back to my soap pads."

I took a breath. "Well, I've heard about how you saw God in church and how they kicked you out, but how did you start healing people?"

Mamaw looked at her hands, still red from hot water, then said, "She give me the gift."

"I know that, but how? Or how did you know?"

Mamaw reached out to smooth the tablecloth. She rearranged the hen and rooster salt and pepper shakers. She straightened paper napkins in their wooden holder. Then she raised her eyes to mine.

"I don't mind to tell it, Lawanda, but how come you all of a sudden want to know?"

So I told her about Jimmy Minniard and how I needed something to say back.

Mamaw put the palm of her hand on her forehead, then slowly moved it down over her face till it rested at her throat.

"First off, I'm sorry about this, Lawanda. Second, you got to know that if you said the whole Book from 'In the beginning' to 'Amen,' it would not change some people's minds. If this Minniard boy's more set on bothering you than hearing the truth, you might as well save your breath."

I knew as soon as she said that that she was right. And I knew something else. "I'd like to hear for myself," I told her.

"That's my girl," she said, and began.

29

MAMAW: "It was hard being turned out of Little Splinter. I was weaned on that church—it was beans and buttermilk to me. Every time there was a service, my mommy had us all there, scrubbed and shiny, with our hair skinned back. I was baptized from that church, married in it, saw my daddy and mommy prayed over there at the once-a-year funeralizing. And biggest thing of all, I saw God Herself in that church, was lifted up just like the old hymn says. And that was the very thing that put me out.

"That Sunday, Lord, I went home so down, I felt I'd never get up again. My sign, which had weighed like the world walking over, I didn't even notice going back.

"Your papaw was out hoeing corn when I got home. He's never been a churchgoer.

" 'What are you doing home early, woman?' he hollered. 'And where are them younguns?'

"Younguns? Upon my honor, I had plumb forgot about them! The service was still going when I was throwed out and I had headed home like a horse to the barn.

"Well, I didn't even speak to your papaw. I pitched my sign into a fencerow and took off up the road a-flying. Halfway there, I met them coming home.

" 'What happened, Mommy?' June cried. 'Where'd you go?'

" 'She was churched,' Burchett said. 'I done told you that.'

"Dolan just stood there with his thumb in his mouth.

" 'Hush, Burchett,' I said, scooping Dolan up with one arm and with the other hugging June to my waist.

" 'Ain't it true?' Burchett insisted.

" 'Can't tell you what's true right now. Let's go home and get some dinner.'

"We did. I watched them all eat hearty while every bite I took tasted like sand.

• • •

"For the next weeks, months, I don't know how long, it seemed like there was a skin over everything. Sun was far away; colors was dimmer. I couldn't even hear good. I'd stand at the stove and not smell dinner burning, not hear your papaw a-calling in the yard.

"Then Annie Isom's boy fell on a wagon tongue and Jeb asked me to sit with her while he went to Cutshin for the doc.

"It was a long journey he was starting, and this boy, Jess, was bleeding real bad. Annie had gone cold and dumb the way people will sometimes. I sent the other younguns to play in the barn. For some cause, I called to Flo as she went out, 'Hunt up a feather and bring it back to me, will you?'

"She did. Brown one, short and wide-splayed, most likely a wren's.

" 'Better put on some coffee, Annie,' I said. 'We'll be needing to keep awake.'

"It was full daylight as I said this, but Annie didn't question, just put more kindling on the fire. I didn't question either. I was following something with my tongue and my hands.

"I went over to the bed where Jess was laying, whiter than just-come snow. Ten years old and his breath on my hand no stronger than a baby's, the sheets wadded around him bright with blood.

" 'Mother Jesus,' I said, something drawing out my voice, 'let us keep Jess, this boy that's just started to grow. Stop his life from spilling. Let his pain fall away like this old wren's feather. Seal his wounds, Mother Jesus, and heal Sister Annie's heart.'

"I had one hand on Jess's forehead as I said this, and with the other I touched the feather to his shoulder bones, the fork of his legs, his heart. I closed my eyes and laid the feather inside my dress, against the heat of my bosom. And I sang:

> 'Leave us a while longer
> In this earthly light.
> Our eyes are not ready
> For Your holy sight.
> Mother, comfort
> Your child and take his ills.
> Leave him to work for you
> Among these sacred hills.'

"I'd never heard this song, mind you, but I heard my voice singing it, hoarse and flat, like wind whining in a door.

"I opened my eyes, and Jess's eyes were open too. A little color had come to his cheeks and the blood on the sheets had darkened. No new came to keep it red.

" 'She's healed him, Annie,' I said. 'Mother Jesus has healed him!'

"Annie rushed over to the bed. She took Jess's hand, stroked his hair, smiled into his face. Then she looked back at me. 'Don't worry, Ada,' she promised. 'I won't never tell.'

• • •

"That seemed a shame at the time, but it didn't really matter. What I knew, I knew, and it closed the church hole in my heart. I won't say I don't sometimes grieve for Little Splinter. But all its members call me when the bad times come. Somebody goes for the doc, somebody for Mamaw. There's been many a door opened to Mother Jesus since Sam Wilder and the church shut us out."

LAWANDA: I couldn't say anything after Mamaw quit. It was bad enough that they'd thrown her out of church because she said she saw God. Isn't that why you go to church? I mean, really? But to find out they took her gift of healing and then pretended it didn't exist— well, it made me want to scream. But I didn't think anybody had ever screamed in that old soft room. So I just said, "Thanks, Mamaw. That's some story."

"I reckon so," she agreed, and got up to go back to the sink. "Would you send your ma in?"

I did, and they spent the rest of the afternoon pinning the pieced top of the quilt to the back and batting. Mom didn't seem to have her mind on it. She kept puckering the top and having to unpin a section and start again. Driving back, she said her nerves were all to pieces with worry about Papaw cleaning fencerows.

"He's seventy-two, you know, Lawanda, and when I told him he should hire one of Jim Creech's boys up the road to do that, he just grunted, 'I'd rather die in the field than in the bed.' "

I stayed tuned in to her talk enough to make the right answers, just as she paid enough attention to the road to make the right turns, but I wasn't really there. I was back in Mamaw's kitchen. "Mother Jesus has healed him," she'd told Annie. Even the words shook me up. If God could be a woman, anything could happen.

• • •

We didn't get back from Little Splinter Creek till almost six, so I made the coleslaw while Mom reheated a pot of pinto beans. We had some biscuits left over from breakfast and a wedge or two of corn bread from dinner.

"Applesauce, Lawanda," Mom ordered from the stove. "Little sweet pickles." That's how she talks when she cooks. I sliced some big yellow onions, too.

I bet it wasn't ten minutes from the time we got in the door till we were all seated at the table: Mom, Dad, Dessie, Jeff, and me. Ray was eating at Uncle Dolan's. He'd been squirrel hunting with Little Jim. Mom set a gallon of buttermilk by my plate and I poured for the kids. Dad put his chin on his collar. "Lord, we thank you for this table full of food and for family to eat it with. Bless the hands that fixed it. Give us the energy and gumption to be good. Amen."

Mom handed him the bread basket, then the beans.

"Speaking of the Lord—" I began, but Mom leaped in.

"Not at the table, Lawanda."

"Dad just did!"

"If you think the food needs more blessing, go right ahead, but I don't want a word about Mother Jesus."

"But Mom—"

Dad was reaching me the coleslaw. "Mind your mother, Lawanda."

My eyes filled with tears and I couldn't get out of there fast enough. They didn't want to hear from Mamaw! They didn't want to hear from me!

"What's wrong with *her*?" Dessie asked as I left the room.

Mom said, "Some people got to wash their corn bread down with tears."

MAMAW: When I got home from that first healing, I fixed supper same as usual. Got the kitchen cleaned up, June, Burchett, and Dolan to bed, then poured some coffee and tried to tell John what had happened. I was still so wound up, I felt like my hands was on fire. He wouldn't hear a word.

"Don't tell me about it," he warned. "You ain't been right since that flash of light ruffled your feathers."

I reminded him he was not the Lord.

"You don't look much like Saving Grace yourself," he said.

"But that's just it," I told him. "I do. She could nurse a youngun. She could *birth* a youngun. God ain't got no pecker. She's like me."

"Ada Marie Holcomb—"

"Listen at that! You're unhitching me just at the thought of it."

"I'm trying to get sense out of you, woman. See if there's any left when you shuck it on down to the cob."

"Shuck your name off me? Go on. But you'll only get my pa's name. My ma's side was Ashers, but that came from her daddy—so you can go on and on and there ain't no cob. I ain't a stalk or a cob or anything that sticks up."

"What are you then?"

36

"Rivers, I reckon. Paths. Watering holes. Places to hide even. Nests."

"Some old broody God you've got, running ever which way."

"No. She don't run. She's plunked herself down at the middle. And she don't ask for war or glory."

"What does she want?"

"People to sing and cook dinner."

"Some God."

"And if you burn the dinner, she's put out. She don't call it sacrifice."

"You just want—"

"What I *want* ain't got nothing to do with it! I'm saying what I seen."

"Yeah? Well, I didn't marry what you seen. I didn't marry some queer woman that turns high-and-mighty because she thinks God got her kicked out of church."

"I ain't being high-and-mighty and you know it. Me having a vision is like June having curly hair. They's good days and bad days, and it don't make you any better than anybody else. It's just a fact, John, like you having that tooth turned wrong."

"There's people that fixes crooked teeth. Maybe there's somebody that can straighten you out."

"No."

"What do you mean 'No'?"

"You I married for all earthly time and I aim to keep true to that: trespass no beds, cook your food, wash your overalls. And I must love you, too, or I never would have put up with you. But I didn't give you ary a promise about what would happen between me and the Lord. It's not mine to give. And not yours to quarrel with."

John shut his eyes. When he opened them, he gave me a look he usually saves for cows. "I can't see why God would pick on you."

"Well, I can't neither unless it's because my head is so empty."

He laughed then and I did, too, and set our coffee cups in the sink so we could get to bed. About a half hour later, I elbowed him in the ribs.

"One thing's for sure," I said.

"What's that?"

"You ain't God!"

We shook the bedsprings laughing that time till we finally snored off to sleep.

LAWANDA: Garland and I could talk about anything; that's what amazed me, once I quit being scared. He never cut me off like my folks did, and while his meanness didn't go away, I figured out it was just a pose, like kids in the hall trying to be cool. He listened too. I could tell him stuff about school I could never tell Mom or Dad—how I didn't fit in and why I had to go to college, not just to get an education but to see something besides Pine Mountain. He said that was fair enough. And I could tell him about Mom and Dad making me so mad. It was like Garland's buses were above it all and when I got up there I could see through his eyes, or at least out his windshield. It helped.

When I told him about Mamaw's first healing, he whistled through his teeth. "Hell of a woman," he said, like it was a holy word. That made me feel better. I'd never thought of Mamaw as strange. She was just Mamaw, the way the wind is the wind.

Garland was such a friend to me and I came to count on him—so much that I didn't see he was changing. Oh, one time I cried and he made me leave, but I didn't see he was starting to count on me too. If I had, I might have guessed that when it came down to it, he'd be worse about me leaving than Mom and Dad.

• • •

The Friday right after my visit with Mamaw, I decided to talk to them about college, share the brochures and catalogs I got in the mail. I waited till the ruckus of supper was over, suggested Mom go watch TV while I cleaned up the mess. Then I asked them if we could talk. Dessie was off with a friend. Ray was trying to teach Jeff a card trick. It seemed like the right time.

It wasn't.

"What's this all about, Lawanda?" Dad asked. And no matter what I told them, how I explained scholarships and applications and my plans, all they would say was, "What's this about?" Oh, they used different words—*money* and *home* and *not rushing into things*—but it all came down to them pretending this was some strange new idea I had. Like we'd never talked about me going away to school, making something out of my life. After an hour, I felt hopeless. It would take a million years to get them to where we could start talking. Ray might as well try to teach Jeff to play bridge.

Finally I just gathered my pile of dreams and said, "You all are tired. Let's talk about this another time." I felt like their mother.

• • •

The only way I could get myself to sleep that night was to think about showing it all to Garland. He'd understand. As much as he's read, he might even know the best place to go.

So after breakfast and chores the next morning, I set off up the hill. I borrowed Dad's jeans jacket with the flannel lining. The grass was spiked with frost and besides, his jacket felt like good luck.

Garland was drinking his second pot of coffee. He poured

some in the Hardee's mug he keeps for me. "Fast food," he said. "Don't stay with you long."

We sat in our usual places in First Bus and I slid my material out of the big Clinch Valley College envelope. Had to use his knees and mine to hold the catalogs. It felt good, like we were conspirators. Then I finished.

"Now see here, Lawanda," Garland began, "I'd like to know what you think you're doing, talking about going to school somewheres far off. We got schools here. You can go to that community college. Jobs is scarce, but you're smart, Lawanda. They'd *give* you money to go to school. What's got you so stuck-up you think you have to leave us?"

"You know it's not that," I told him.

"I don't know nothing but that you're looking to haul your fool self over the ridge."

"Garland . . ." I looked at him, trying to find what I might say that he'd listen to.

"Well?" All of a sudden, I didn't see him fierce and barrel-chested. I saw an old, hairy baby.

"Everybody leaves when they get out of high school if they mean to make something of themselves."

"That's the stupidest thing you've said yet."

"But it's true."

"Oh, yeah, I know. They roll right out of here like them high-piled coal cars, and that's one more load of heat and light we ain't got."

"I didn't say I wouldn't come back."

He glared at me, tightened his full red face.

"Nobody has to spell *sun* to me, Lawanda. I know what comes up of a morning."

Well, I'd just about had it. Dad, Mom, everybody was on me. And now Garland. I thought he'd be on my side. What did he have to do with it anyway?

"What the hell has it got to do with you?"

41

When I said that, something snapped in the air like the recoil from cutting tight wire. Garland grabbed the wheel of the bus and pulled his weight around to stare out the windshield. All he could see was a wall of sky and the rear end of Second Bus. I waited. He sat there, stony as the mountain.

I was still mad and at the same time I wanted to get up and put my hands on his shoulders, to take it all back. "You are two people, Lawanda," I said to myself. "Theirs and yours. If you ever expect to get out of here, stay put." So I did. But I apologized.

"Okay, Garland, I'm sorry. I shouldn't have said that. But you don't know how it is. Every time I open my mouth, somebody's onto me. Every idea I have, they wad up like so much trash. I'm fifteen years old—did you ever think of that? I can't stay with Mom and Dad forever. I can't spend my life with Mamaw. I've got to be going somewhere."

"This bus don't roll."

"I know that."

"So don't think if you go away you can just come back."

"Why not?"

"I'm alive, Lawanda." He was still facing the windshield.

"I know that too."

"You can go off and leave a bus but a person needs tending to." He closed his eyes.

"Now what's that supposed to mean?" I was getting mad again. I stood up. He just sat there. "Come on, Garland. I'm not a well you can drop your thoughts into. What are you talking about?"

Nothing.

"Look at me!" I was practically screaming.

"All right, goddamn it! Sit down." He turned around. "You!" he said, like it was a filthy thing rolled to the front of his mouth. "Fifteen years old! Baby Moses going to crawl to the Promised Land. You make me sick."

"Thanks."

"Don't get sassy with me, Lawanda Ingle."

"You're not my daddy."

"How do you know?"

He leaned forward in his seat, the leather cracking. A woody smell of whiskey rode his breath. I leaned back. Dad had said he was dangerous. Was he crazy?

"My daddy's Howard Ingle. You know that."

He narrowed his hard blue eyes.

"You make me want to puke."

"It's your bus," I told him.

"Yeah, and you're in it. The best thing in it. And that's how I like it, Lawanda."

Fear went through my stomach like a knife.

"And I like to be here," I said. "But I'm not a book, Garland. Not something you can order and keep." He belched. "I'm not a bottle either."

I stood up. So did he. I started to turn toward the door, but his hands came down on my shoulders. He hardly had to push at all and I sat down.

"Listen to me, Lawanda."

"Okay," I said, "but I can't stay long."

"Ain't that what we're talking about?"

I nodded.

"You're scared," he said.

"Maybe." I stared right into his cold red-threaded eyes. "Not as scared as you."

"Aarrglch!" He made this sound like he had the worst chest cold in the world. He put one big hand over his face.

"Garland?" Oh God, I thought, he can't be going to cry. He took his hand down and looked at me.

"Baby girl," he said, "I've lost more than you've ever heard of. Go on home now. Come back when you've got something to say besides good-bye."

TWO

JUNE: Something's bothering that girl.
Now she's gone off up the hill with Mommy. What a pair:
Lawanda, who thinks the world will open its arms, and
Mommy, who believes God already did. I don't know what
to think about it.

Now I have always loved my mommy, and not just because I had to. But it's not been easy. Kids teased me from
the time Mommy got churched about her being crazy and
traipsing off to heal people.

"Junie thinks God lives at her house!" Eddie Duff would
holler.

"And wears an apron!" somebody would throw in. I never
mentioned it to Mommy.

Pap said to pay them no mind. "World's full of people
who can't tend to their own business." I wanted to ask him
what *he* thought about Mother Jesus, but I knew better.
That was between him and Mommy. He'd never let it out.

So I still wonder. Pap's not had it easy. Been rode hard
and put up wet most of his life. Mommy was what he had,
his comforter. Sharing her with us younguns—well, we
didn't rob what she gave him. Leastways, that's how it's
been with Howard and me. Love for my kids just makes
me love their daddy more. But if I got crazy over God like
Mommy did—why, it'd be worse than if I took up with

some other man! Who could go to bed with the Lord there between you? I never could reckon it.

If they fought over this, I didn't hear it. Maybe Pap was out plowing down angels in the field; maybe they wrestled after they packed us all off to school. Ada and John. Set out tobacco together, suckered it, hoed and weeded and topped it. Raised corn and beans and potatoes, kept a cow and pigs, raised hay. Worked sunup to sundown and then some. "And still not past going," Pap says.

Which is true, but sometimes I think he's getting close. Not in the body. He's kept moving, so he's not froze up like a lot of folks his age. It's his mind that worries me. Like the other Sunday when we were setting on the porch, talking about how pretty the leaves were, about Ray out squirrel hunting, and out of nowhere Pap said, "That would have been in the Great War."

"What, Pap?"

"The way it was with phone books. Well, you wouldn't remember."

"No," I said, my insides seized up. I waited a minute or two and he just gazed off at the gold-and-red hillside. Then I said, "Pap, we weren't talking about the war just now."

His eyes flickered at me. Did he know he'd gone off?

"Two sides to a conversation," he said.

When I brought this up to Mommy, she laid it on work. "He's tired is all," she said. "I try to get him not to work so hard, but I might as well tell winter not to come."

So there you are. Pap and Mommy are as closed off from me as when I was a little girl. And Lawanda's found her own world, too. You belong to yourself and your husband, I guess. Can't expect much else. You're lucky if you've got that. Sure looks promising when you have those babies, though.

Now here's Lawanda reaching out to Mommy. What does Mommy know about the world Lawanda lives in? Can a feather scare up college for Lawanda? Can it save her from her own foolishness? Where smart don't get to, Lawanda's real stupid. And stubborn! Stubbornest creature ever born, except Mommy and Howard Ingle. Her and Mommy are a good match in that.

Lord knows what they're doing up there, roaming the ridge like it was May, not November, Mommy with only a rag of a sweater. Lawanda never thinks of that. She never thinks how Mommy's no spring chicken. Mommy don't either. She'll drop dead canning or cleaning fencerows or driving these hills at night, calling her headlights Mother Jesus' eyes.

I don't know what to do with either one of them—except put on some coffee to thaw them out when they get home.

LAWANDA: I have to tell you I was shook up about Garland. I'm not sure what I was scared of except that he might not let me get away from First Bus. I was mad at him too. Why did he have to spoil things?

At the same time, somehow I hurt for Garland. He wasn't like I thought, strong and sealed off in himself. No, he was suffering and I didn't know why.

I couldn't ask him. I was scared to go up there again.

For days I kept turning this over. I could just stay away, but I missed his company. I could tell Mom and Dad, but that would be the end of that. Who could I talk to? Finally I settled on Mamaw.

I didn't see her again till right before Thanksgiving, when she came over to take my cousin Trula to the dentist and I put it to her.

"Mamaw, let's take a walk."

"On *this* road? The coal trucks'll run us down."

"No, up the hill behind the house. I want to show you something, see what you think it is."

That pleased her. Mamaw is our plant namer.

Halfway up the path, she asked, "This thing a tree or a herb?"

"Neither one."

50

"What's on your mind, Lawanda? You're looking peaked."

"It's a long story. Let's go on up to the laurel rock and sit down."

We did. Mamaw has this amazing way of sitting with a big hand turned palm up on each knee. She looks like she's waiting for something from heaven. Probably is.

"I'm listening," she said. And the story coiled so tight in me unrolled like a lock of hair.

Mamaw's face didn't change. Once or twice she put a hand up to shade her eyes. Then when I was finished, she said, "You been praying about this?"

I shook my head.

"Then I reckon it must be him."

"What?"

"Doing the praying."

"Garland? He wouldn't ever—"

"Hush, Lawanda. First off, you've just proved you don't know this feller. And second, praying don't have to mean getting on your knees."

"What does it mean then?"

"Prayer is whatever you do in the direction of God."

"Mamaw . . ." This wasn't helping a bit.

"You know how a plant you set in a window will grow toward the sun?"

"Yes ma'am."

"That's prayer."

I studied on that a minute. And on Mamaw, fierce and soft, sitting on the rock slab, her blue housedress faded as the sky.

"When it came right down to it," she went on, "your friend turned toward the light."

"Came down to what? I thought he'd be glad for me."

"Amos Garland is an old, old man."

"Amos? He said his name was Garland, first and last."

"Well, it's Amos."

"And he's not much older than you, is he?"

"I'm not talking about years, Lawanda. I'm talking about how much a person has been worn away."

She took off her glasses, blew on each lens, then cleaned them on her dress tail.

"I never really knew Amos, but I was friends with his sister Chloe. She kept store at Redbird when I was a new-married woman. Lord a mercy, Chloe was pretty. Men would come plumb across Pine Mountain just to look at her. Then they'd feel foolish and buy a sack of nails or a little box of peppermint sticks."

Mamaw stopped to collect her thoughts, and a cardinal called down the ridge. *Who's here? Who's here?*

"Ain't that pretty? Who's here? Who's here?" she called back. Then she was quiet.

"Mamaw?"

"What, Junie?"

"It's Lawanda. Mamaw, are you getting cold?"

"I reckon I am. This rock's found my rheumatiz."

"Let's climb up a ways farther and walk the ridge in the sun."

Helping her up, I felt ashamed that I'd been troubling over Garland while my grandmother sat listening, stiff with cold.

"Amos was in the war," Mamaw began when we were up in a little clearing. " 'In heavy fighting.' That's all he wrote to Chloe. His wife said he was wounded, decorated, and sent right back to the front. I don't recall which ocean he crossed. He wasn't a young man either. Amos had been a schoolteacher, married, with his own younguns. Most likely, the army wouldn't have called him, but for some cause he wanted to go.

"I remember when Chloe heard he was coming home. She had a flag in the window, put streamers up in the store. 'Welcome home, hero!' she printed on butcher paper, made a banner to go above the door.

"Nora was his wife, and Chloe went with her to Cardin to meet the bus. After they watched everybody get off and didn't see him, they asked the driver if there was a soldier asleep on the bus.

" 'That there's our only soldier,' the driver told them. And he pointed to a heap of rags leaned against the wall.

"Garland?" I asked her.

"Chloe said he was skin and bones and he stank. 'Like a dog in a cage.' And he acted wild, too. Tore Chloe's banner down with one paw, shouting, 'Hero? Then tell me why I ain't dead.'

"Drunk was what he was, drunk and dirty. And when she bathed him, Nora said he was all over scars.

"What happened to her?"

"Chloe or Nora? Nora was a wife to him for as long as she could be. He was sweet sometimes, but he was crazy, Lawanda. Couldn't hold a job, couldn't let the kids out of his sight. Once Nora came home from the store and found Delbert chained to the bed. Eight years old and his daddy had him in chains.

"Finally, Nora took the younguns and left."

"Left him crazy?"

"Not before he tried to kill her. Thought she was the enemy sneaking up in his sleep.

"After she was gone, it looked like he'd come and live with Chloe. Then *she* got shot—"

"I can't believe this," I told her.

"Nobody else could either. A man who'd been driving from La Follette just to buy cornmeal shot her in the head. Said she'd promised for years to run off with him. Nobody even knew his name. That's when Amos went to live in the bus."

"Where did he get the buses?"

"Second one's a ruined city bus. The first one, the school board sold him cheap."

"And he had children?"

"Lord, yes. Let's see, there was Ardith and Delbert and Nancy Catherine, and then a baby who came after the war. I remember Chloe being so scared for that baby. . . ." Mamaw shook her head. "He's probably got grandchildren by now. Could be your age. Amos is only a year or two older than me."

"Where are they?"

"I don't know. Don't know if anyone does." She stopped a minute. "I reckon that's why he claims you."

MAMAW: I didn't say this to Lawanda,

but I knew after our talk I'd have to go see Amos. I just told her to wait, give me time to think.

Driving back to Little Splinter Creek I wished for the old road, gravel path alongside the creek. I like to ride rough when I'm doing hard thinking. Like the wheel to pull against. That smooth tongue of a road we got now can sail you along like you was singing and you headed down the gullet of a big mistake.

Trula was numb and sleepy. She'd had her sweet tooth silvered.

For some cause, what came to me was the night Lawanda was born. Noonie and Ray had both been struggles—one big-headed and the other one backward—but a couple of hours' solid work and Lawanda was here. June couldn't believe it.

"You sure it's all done?" she kept asking Doc Combs. "Afterbirth and everything?"

"All's left for you to do is name her, and you can wait on that."

But June had already settled on Lawanda, "with no middle name to mess it up."

That baby was a sight—long-legged, smiling, and hungry for the world. Hasn't changed a bit.

Lord, when I think of such a child on that mountain in that bus. And I knew she'd go back. She's got a big heart. Hearing Garland's story, she'd want to reach out to him. And then she's curious, the kind of youngun who has to see what makes fire burn. She'd go back. I just had to be sure I got there first.

The trouble was, it was Thanksgiving week when she told me, and all the kids was due in, plus John's brother Ed from over at Dwarf. I'd have to climb a mountain of potatoes and swim a river of gravy before I could get off the Creek again. So I called Lawanda up when I got home. I'm not much for the telephone but I will use it if I have to. I said what was true, that she should hold off another week or so before seeing Garland, just to let things settle. And I told John I'd need to go to Cardin right after Thanksgiving to fetch cake makings.

"I thought you did your trading yesterday," John said. "Ain't you got a brain?"

"That was for Thanksgiving," I told him. "This is for Christmas."

Now I couldn't go on Friday because Burchett and his family was leaving up in the day, and I always make them a turkey pie to take home. But Saturday morning, right after milking, I set out.

I did stop at Fraley's for flour and sugar and dried apples in case I didn't have enough. Then I drove the Hallspoint Road at the bottom of Amos's hill. Parked the Plymouth almost in a ditch.

A wind had come up and the light was thin. Lord, I felt old, headed up that hill. Kept thinking how warm Chloe's kitchen used to be.

There was nobody in what I made out to be First Bus. Neat as a pin, just like Lawanda said. But it was padlocked. I walked through the broken garden. Not enough cornstalks to hide in. I went around to Second Bus.

I could see Amos through the door. He was asleep in the

aisle, zipped into a sleeping bag like some huge caterpillar in its cocoon. Back seats had been taken out, but for some cause he didn't sleep there. I could see a table, clothes, some kitchen stuff. The bus was awful trashy. The glass box for fares was full of cigarette butts.

I knocked.

Nothing.

I pounded.

He groaned and put his forearm over his eyes.

I called out to him.

"Amos! Amos Garland!"

He muttered something and sat up. His face hurt to look at it.

Crawling out of the army bag, getting to his feet and wrapping it around him, he stood up and stumbled toward the door.

Yanking at the lever to open it, he said, "Who in grease-splattered Hell are you?"

"Ada Smith, Lawanda's mamaw."

"Oh, no." His face knotted.

"We need to talk."

He looked and looked at me. Finally he said, "Other bus. Give me a minute."

So I turned and eased off the high steps. I looked down the hill. The Plymouth could have been a green rag about to blow down to the creek. I thought how I could still catch it, still head back to Little Splinter. . . .

"All right, Mamaw." Amos was dressed now—greasy jeans, flannel shirt—and carrying a coffee can. "This way."

He handed me the can while he undid the lock.

"I'll get the heater going," he said. "This bus gets colder than kraut."

So I followed him in. It was just like Lawanda said—books and maps, everything neat as a pin. He showed me where to sit, turned the heater on.

"Amos—" I started.

"I know why you're here."

"I knew your sister."

"Dead and gone," he said, and headed toward the back of the bus.

"I helped lay her out."

"Prettied her up for the send-off?" He raised his eyebrows at me. "Kind of hard, weren't it, with that hole in her head?"

I went down the aisle.

"Don't lay any hands on me." He was measuring coffee with a bent-lipped spoon.

"Amos—"

"Say that one more time and I'll show you where I keep my gun."

"Garland, then."

"Now and ever shall be." He poured water into the pot from a plastic jug.

"I know you lost Nora—"

"You know too much."

"And your children—"

"Little snakebites."

"And I know that makes Lawanda—"

"You don't know nothing about Lawanda."

"I saw her born."

"Saw Chloe out. Saw Lawanda in. What are you, some kind of doorkeeper?"

"What are you?"

"I'm a drunk."

"What else?"

"Ain't that enough?"

"No."

"I'm a mean old man."

"What else?"

The water was starting to boil, shoot brown jets into the glass knob.

"Baccer juice," he said. "A mouthful of baccer juice."

"God's own creature," I told him.

58

"Then God done some pretty poor work."

"And Lawanda—how'd She do on Lawanda?"

"Oh, Lawanda's a guest of the world," he said.

"You think Lawanda don't know hardship?"

"She don't know much."

"She knows what it's like to be hungry."

"Good. She's alive."

"She knows what it's like to be scared sick by somebody you love."

"You want some of this?" He held up the battered pot. "The cups ain't exactly clean."

"If it's hot, I'll take it."

The cup was white with green lines around the rim, a truck-stop cup.

"Milk?" he asked, holding up a can of Pet milk.

I shook my head. "You sure are civilized," I told him.

"More'n when I lived in a house."

I followed him up the aisle, grateful for a cup to hold to.

"Lawanda—" I started.

"Lawanda's dead."

"*She is not.* She—"

"I don't want to hear no more about her."

"All she wants—"

"She wants all everybody wants and nobody gets, and I can't stand to look at it."

"Oh."

"You preachers got any respect for that?"

"I'm no preacher."

"What are you then?"

"An old woman."

"What else?"

"I got a gift, if that's what you mean."

"A gift?" he said, raking the fingers of his right hand through his beard. "Ain't that dandy?"

"Sometimes it's awful."

"God tries to get you to haul ass to Nineveh?"

59

"Or thereabouts," I told him.

"She's like you."

"Who?"

"Her we ain't talking about."

"She's like you, too," I said.

He looked like he might throw the coffee in my face. Instead, he said, "So tell me about Nineveh, and don't leave out the whale."

And I told him. Everything from the vision to being churched to learning I was a healer. Seemed like he didn't bat an eye.

"You ever see her again, this woman Jesus?"

"Not like that first time."

"Don't it make you wonder?"

"What?"

"Well, you could've had a stroke."

"Maybe so, but I didn't."

"You got any of them feathers with you?"

"What for?"

"You ever heal pictures?"

"Pictures?"

"Yeah," he said. His eyes were heating up now. "Let's see your plumage, Mamaw."

I can't say why I did it—it goes against everything—but I reached in my coat and into my dress front and took out a wing feather from a quail.

"God's elbows!" he said.

"Could be."

"You wait here," he told me.

Heavy and old as he was, he made a beeline for Second Bus. The draft from his leaving hadn't died down till he was coming back through the door.

He had a shoe box.

He sat down with it on his knees. I'd have give more than I can say not to have seen what was in it.

Pictures, like he'd said. Old ones—his mommy and

60

daddy, I guess. One of him in his uniform, one of Nora, a wedding picture, and then God's plenty of the younguns— baby pictures, school pictures, one from the paper when Delbert won the spelling bee. Every one of them had the face burnt out.

I breathed in hard.

"That's what I do to what leaves," he said.

"You must have left, too, then. Your face is burnt out."

He stood up.

"Here," he said, shoving the box in my lap. "Call up your spirits."

"You've done called up yours," I told his back as he went down the aisle.

"Ever take whiskey in your coffee?" he asked me.

I don't cry, but that's where I would have started.

"No."

"Take it straight?"

"No."

"Shame to drink alone," he declared, coming back up the aisle.

"You seem to manage."

He sat down.

"I do with what I got."

I ran my hand through the pictures like they was leaves.

"I can't look at this," I told him.

"My burnt-out people?"

"You with that bottle."

"You know your way down the hill."

"Yes sir, and I know the way you're going."

"Feet first," he said.

"And not a heart in you."

"What's that supposed to mean?"

"Means you're trying to drown it, burn it away."

"Ain't your feathers going to fix that?"

"Make the faces come back? Not if you'd rather see labels on a bottle."

"I'd sure rather look at Jack Daniel's than you."

"Comes as no surprise."

"What does? What does surprise you, Mamaw? You're about as even-tempered as a rock."

"I'm surprised you let my girl off this hill with nothing split but her heart."

"God Almighty!"

"That's what I told her, that God was protecting her up here, where she knew she shouldn't ought to have come."

"You are one stinking old woman! Who do you think I am?"

"Somebody who don't see the light, and it shining on him."

He grunted. "That's a pretty thing to say." He tilted the bottle and drank. "But it don't put faces on my pictures."

"You have one of Lawanda?"

"No."

"That's good. Thank you for the coffee."

"You going to give me one?"

"No. But you can have the feather."

I put it in the picture box and handed it over.

"Mother Jesus, huh? You reckon they nailed Her up in a skirt?"

I stood by the steps, my hand on the silver pole.

" 'The Lord stood upon a wall made by a plumb line,' " I recited, " 'with a plumb line in his hand.' "

"What's that?"

"Amos," I said. "The Prophet."

"Flap them Bibles, jiggety-jig."

"All I'm saying is, we're measured. However you been praying, keep it up."

"Not me!" he boasted.

"I bet that garden gets you on your knees," I told him.

He laughed a big long braying laugh. It followed me on a thin wind down to the road.

GARLAND: Mad old woman goes off and leaves me with this box. I watch her, then turn and steady myself, putting my hand on the heater. Hot as God's tongue. Blisters my hand so, I can hardly hold the box or a bottle. Never had a woman cross my doorsill but brought bad luck.

Nora: hardest-hearted, softest-bodied woman I ever run into. Didn't care for me once she had them younguns. Picked my pockets clean.

Chloe: the biggest gift God give her was a ticket to her own funeral. Face like a heart. Man drives up, breaks it with a shotgun. The rest of her still smooth as a snake.

My own girls, Ardith and Nancy Catherine, dancing and singing: now why? Their mommy scared, their daddy no account. They'd go on making songs for their clothespin dolls. I hit my girls. I had to. World's too hard.

And then Lawanda. Hikes up here, Miss Priss, with a hammer for my heart. I don't care a whit about her. Don't ever want to see her fuzzy blond face again.

She's smart, Lawanda is. She's tough. But she shouldn't never have climbed this hill. If she was mine, I wouldn't allow it.

And sending her mamaw—big old slap-jawed woman! No, Lawanda didn't do that. She must have told her mamaw,

63

though. Knowing Chloe. Mamaw's big hands on Chloe's flesh.

Footlocker. Coffin. Bus. Give me a jailhouse. Send me somewhere, you officers of the law! Am I going to rot up here? Are you leaving me to do my worst?

I got their faces. I don't need them on these pictures. They're burnt into me is what it is. I see them every time I close my eyes. Used to see them in the bottom of a glass. Now I just drink out of the bottle.

Okay. I ain't so pitiful. They's worse than me. I could go to town if I took a mind to. I got better pants than this. I could go see Curtis Ballard. Where's he got to, anyway? And if Howard Ingle was there . . .

I don't want to think about Howard Ingle. Nor his daughter. Nor his Bible-mouthed mother-in-law. God's plumb line! I reckon it drops straight down to Hell.

And everything in between's so crooked, it makes that plumb line look like a guy wire. Yep. A guy wire for Satan's telephone pole. Call me up, Old Scratch, you hot number. We'll fry the bird feet. We'll burn the whole box here— Nora's whelps and Mamaw's breast feather.

But hold off till this evening. Right now, I got to go to town.

● ● ●

That Mamaw's done sprung me from my bus without a bite to eat. Aw, hell, my digestion's ruint anyway. Belly burns and every mouthful I send down is just fuel for the fire.

Coffee and whiskey, I can tolerate—that's about it. And a real hard apple. Most other stuff, you can have. And me with a garden big enough to feed the five thousand.

Nothing left now but broccoli and collards. I done decapitated my cabbage the first of last week. Rolled their little heads into a hole I dug. No cellar in a bus.

I ought to take Curtis Ballard some of them cabbages. Make him a mean slaw. Sit down with that and some beans, a pone of bread . . . well, Curtis has got people to sit down *with*. Me, I don't want nobody.

So I'll tell him to come on up to the place and get him a head or two. Why should I have to haul the things to town? I'm no peddler. A good thing, too. I couldn't sell water to a man whose house was afire.

Lawanda, now, she sold me them magazines. One music, one science. You'd think they'd be real different. Nah, they're both full of numbers. Gives me the headache.

Where'd they put that town anyway? Thing is, I started out the long way, I think. Yeah, I did. Didn't want to crash into them Ingles. No sir. That Mamaw's a Mack truck. Fact is, I don't want to see a living creature but Curtis. Shut my eyes to them squirrel-hunting boys back there. Sure don't want to see no woman. Harlots riding the beast, every one of them.

Somebody ought to mow this mountain, clear-cut it, bush-hog it. How's a man supposed to walk with sawbriers and saplings snatching at his legs? Why don't the earth grow roads? You ever think of that? It grows rivers, don't it? Me, I think the Creator was flat-out drunk. By the time He got to us, anyway. I mean, if you'd done made dark and light, and thought up land and water, if you'd got the life spark started and then fired it off into everything from lizards to tobacco plants, wouldn't you want a drink?

It was the weekend, anyway. Friday night, let's break out the jug and make man. Or maybe it was Saturday and He was hungover like a wet blanket on a fence. That'd account for why we're so puny and hateful. God being who He says and all, can you think about what a headache He'd get? You reckon on that next time you look in a mirror. Might tell you something.

I swear my knees is giving out. It's the pitch of this ground, sliding and grabbing. And my shoe sole catching on rocks or sticks and peeling back like a tongue. I could do with hooves, I'm telling you.

There it is, the little town of Cardin. Looks like hair in an armpit. Stinks, too. You ever notice how everything people makes has to shit sooner or later? And they go right on acting like it don't. Might as well not diaper a youngun. I ain't even down there and I want to go home already.

No, I don't. I want to walk into We-Suit-U. I want to see Curtis Ballard in his own bus.

Cold, though. Radio weather. Kids used to listen. "Good morning," it would say. "Good morning, I'm the Christmas Bear." Chained to a voice. Sit in a circle. Go anywhere. So I threw it out, all of them crying.

Aw, God, it don't do to think about it.

A red light. Look, hanging there, swinging. And people stop for that contraption. They turn on their blinkers and wait.

Lock their doors, too. Polish their shoes. Ain't it pitiful?

I know where We-Suit-U is. I used to get clothes dry-cleaned. I worked in this town, got my pay, my zippers zipped. At home I had a bedful of kids and a wife.

I even been in the bank. Used to go regular. None of that green wadded in a sock for me. Going to rise above.

Good thing I brought this pint. Curtis might be thirsty. I don't drink on the street, mind you. They's a billboard I can go behind over at the gas station.

Might as well pee while I'm here.

• • •

"What do you mean, who am *I*? Who are *you*, you big, white, ugly thing? You can't haul me in for bodily functions.

"Yeah, well, I ain't got the key to their goddamn rest room.

"I'm telling you, I don't need a policeman. I *got* somewhere to go. The We-Suit-U cleaners. Going to visit Curtis Ballard, a friend of mine. Long time. You call him. You . . ."

GALT: Now we're into it. Now we're
really into it, boys, and I don't know who's going to get
out. I been a jailer a long time and the way I see it, we get
two kinds of clients: the dangerous, who pass through once,
and the regulars, who come and go like family. This Garland's been one of those. Obnoxious, but not a threat—
that's what I would have said.

I guess I respected him, too, because he taught me back
in school—civics and English. His mind was sharp as a tack
then, and his tongue, too. Young and smart and powerful
good-looking—already married with kids when the war
came. But he joined up. Some folks said it was because the
army'd called his brother Elias and the two wanted to go
together. I don't know. Anyway, they weren't in the same
unit. And Elias didn't come back.

So Garland's had his share of grief. And he traded his
family for a bottle, I know that. But I thought he wasn't
hurting anybody but himself. Now I don't know.

Soon as he quit wailing and shaking the bars last night,
he commenced worrying about his bus. I thought he was
just paranoid with the d.t.'s, but he kept saying he'd left the
place unlocked and his whole life was in there. Wouldn't I
just send somebody up Cade's Hill, he said, and not leave
it open overnight? Hell, I thought, nobody'd steal books,

but it might calm the critter down. So I dispatched Terry Sizemore. Thought he'd be back inside of an hour. I was getting right worried by the time he rolled in.

Turned out the old man had reason to be afraid. Some Messer boys from up Hallspoint Road had not only got in the bus but built a fire in the middle of the skids. Feeding it with books and reading one, too. Hooting and carrying on, drinking whiskey they'd brought or found. Lucky for Garland he had water jugs at the back of the bus, so Terry doused the blaze. Then he brought the boys and their reading matter down to me.

Now none of the Messers has phones, so after making the boys scrub a cell apiece, I had Terry haul them back to their daddy. The news was off by then, so I just sat down and flipped through Garland's book. Spiral, three sections, like he used to make us buy for class.

First two sections was filled with whiskery writing. I looked at the pages the boys had been reading—you could tell by the smudges and drools. There was a whole page about how beans grow, about vines and veins and chromosomes. Shit, I thought, that's what happens when you live alone. Then came a part about black holes in space and then, I swear, two pages about his bus being a tank going to come down and save the town. From what? No wonder them boys was a-bellowing.

But so far so good. I won't fault a man who thinks he's a pole bean or a rocket or a hero. It's batty, but if you want to live in a school bus with nothing to nurse but Ezra Brooks, that's your lookout. Then I flipped into section three.

That's where I found it, boys, the part that burned off my eyelids, the part that's going to singe many an ear. Don't think I don't feel sorry for Howard Ingle. And his dirty daughter. I told him that on the phone. But what's putrid has to come out, I say, or there's no healing. And when it does, it could lock Garland in a jail a lot bigger than this.

CURTIS: Galt called me first thing

Monday morning to say he had Garland in jail. He sounded all wound up but wouldn't say over what, so I took my lunchtime to go find out.

Now I look at people sort of like I look at cloth. It may come to you stained and twisted, snagged or singed, and your first job is to see it for what it is. Then ask questions to find out how it got that way. This is before you *do* anything. You may think you can tell cherry pie filling from blood, but that's not always the case. Of course, the person carrying in the clothes won't always tell you either.

A dress, a suit—it's personal. After all, it's your second skin. Lie about one to save your neck and you'll lie about the other. Human nature.

But Garland doesn't lie, not in my book. More likely, he'll tell you truths you wish you hadn't heard. I thought about this walking up Fox Street that gray first day of December. I've thought about it since. Seems like we make some folks bear our stories we don't want to think about. The war, for instance. I wasn't there; I can have a clean, clear version, if the soldiers will just keep quiet. Then men like Garland, the ones who paid the price, can go on paying it.

Anyhow, I picked up some hot dogs from the drugstore. I'd hate to be dependent on Galt to fill my plate.

The jail was cold and dingy. Urine and Pine Sol scoured my nose.

"I hope you got some powerful solvent," Garland said as Galt fumbled for the key.

"You need cleaning?"

"Boiled in oil and baptized in blood," he said.

"How's your digestion?"

"Fair," he answered, spitting at the drain in the middle of the floor. "They don't give me nothing worth metabolizing."

"No liquor, either?"

"Not a living drop. I'm hoping Father Connor will bring the Communion cup."

I let that pass and handed him the hot dogs. He unwrapped one, broke it in two, and gave me half.

"So you were pissing and boozing behind the Valvoline sign?" I said.

"What goes in must come out."

"That's not pretty," I told him, "but it doesn't sound very criminal to me."

"It's practically holy next to what they're charging me with."

"What's that?"

"Endangering a minor."

"What?"

"Threatening corruption."

I began to wonder if he was paranoid from the d.t.'s.

"Garland, I don't know what you're talking about."

"It's who," he said, a shiver running over him. "It's Lawanda Ingle."

"Not Howard's girl?"

"The same."

My heart sank. "What's she got to do with you?"

"She came to see me."

"So?"

70

"She's fifteen years old."

"When?"

"When what?"

"When did she come to see you?"

"All fall. First she showed up in my garden, selling magazines."

"What did you do to her?"

"I bought some."

"That's not endangerment."

"That's not all."

"Go on."

I waited for him to explain. He sat hunched forward on the bunk, his big belly shrunken in his shirt like a cantaloupe after frost.

"Think Father Connor would bring me some prayers?"

"Do you want one?"

"No."

"Then go on."

"I didn't do anything to her. Well, I got mad at her a couple of weeks ago, talking about going away to school."

"Why?"

"She has no cause to go off and leave me."

"Garland . . ." I felt around for words. "You're not her daddy."

"No. But she's fixing to leave him too."

"That's what kids do when they grow up."

"Lawanda's not grown!"

"Well, it's part of growing—"

"Anyway, I got mad. And she left and I haven't seen her since."

"So?"

"But I wrote about her."

This statement stood and stretched itself before it kicked me in the gut.

"Wrote what?"

"Stuff."

"Do you have it?"

"*They* have it."

"Did you give it to them?"

"No, goddamn it! They broke into my bus! They laid waste my property! They read in my book!"

"I don't know if that's legal."

"That don't matter. The law can't break the law."

Fierce as he was, Garland looked pale, cornered. It was catching. Oh God, I thought, get me back to the dry cleaner's. Give me something I can smooth out, stains I can remove.

"Buddy," Garland said, his voice down from its rage. "You look sick."

A big fist of spit plugged my throat.

"Aye, gonnies!" he exclaimed, and sent out a dazzling wad for both of us. "The world's no fit place to live."

On impulse, I took his hand—not just rested mine on and above it but laced my fingers with his.

"I believe you," I said.

"I wouldn't," he grumbled in return.

Not till Galt let me out and I turned to wave did Garland lift his hand and show the blistered palm.

I started to exclaim, but he just laughed. "I got tired of reading the same old palm," he said. "Thought I'd burn it off and start me another life."

LAWANDA:

Dear Garland,

I heard at school about you being in jail and the Messer boys breaking in First Bus. I'm really sorry. I'll go up and check on things if you want.

I want you to know I am not mad anymore. You just surprised me is all, right when I needed somebody on my side. But it'll be two years before I go to college. Can't we be friends in the meantime?

I have made some money baby-sitting and I got you this harmonica. I figured you were missing yours.

Take care of yourself. I hope Galt makes good coffee. See you when you get out.

Your friend,
Lawanda

P.S. I had to tell Dad I knew you to get him to give this to Mr. Ballard to bring you. I am not in a good light.

HOWARD: I got a bad taste in my
mouth—metal and burning, like I touched a live wire. On
top of everything, Lawanda gives me this letter, gives it to
me for Garland, saying, "I know you think he's bad, but
he's my friend." When I said, "You weren't supposed to
set foot up there," she just answered, "A person has to have
her own friends. Anyway, I told Mamaw."

"Then what?" I asked her.

"She said not to see him for a while and I haven't."

If this wasn't so awful, I would have got mad at her then,
but I am pure past it. I just took the note and the mouth
harp and said, "I don't know, Lawanda."

She don't know either. She thinks they're keeping him
locked up because of the liquor—she don't dream it has to
do with her.

I feel like I been whittling on the front porch while the
baby's room was afire.

Being crazy don't excuse nobody. Right mind or wrong,
Garland could have killed Lawanda or taken her crazy with
him, like that bus rolling off the hill.

Which it hasn't, but I keep seeing it happen, keep thinking
I'd like to push it off myself.

Filthy place! Filthy old drunkard's mind!

Galt won't let me read what Garland wrote. Says it's

74

evidence "for the court's eye alone. But it'll make your hair curl," he told me. "It'll just about stop your heart."

I want to go up to the schoolhouse and collar that principal and say, Who do you think you are, sending these younguns out to sell magazines? Ain't you ever heard of the world? But the school didn't send her. It was Lawanda's idea. And I let her go.

But I'd already forbid her to go up to Garland's! Warned her a long time ago. You can't tie your children in the house, can't leash them to the bedpost.

And I want to shake the feathers out of that Ada Smith. She knew! Lawanda talked to her! And did Mamaw come to me, Lawanda's daddy, the one responsible? No. She just takes it in. Offers it to Mother Jesus and tells Lawanda to stay home. Like telling a river to stop rolling, that there's a waterfall around the next bend.

And Junie. Junie's got her hands full with the house and the other kids, trying to stretch money and clothes and food. She don't even know about this. Never has been able to reckon with Lawanda anyway.

So it's me that knows and has to deal. I go around and around—I run and fall back, a dog going to break the chain or die.

What about Curtis Ballard? He's Garland's friend, has been to see him at the jail. For years he's fed the old man, carried plants to his garden. What would he say to the crop that's come up there now?

Raising the devil in the rows of his book. Big notebook, Galt said, big as the eighth-grade speller.

Aye Lord, and my Lawanda's in there! What can I say to her? I'd about worked something out and then she handed me this baby letter. Who's tricking who? It's a shame I wasn't the one that broke in Garland's bus. If for some cause he ever got out of jail, there'd be nothing left for him to go home to.

FATHER CONNOR: I set off to see
Amos in jail with a heavy heart. And some holy oil. He
can't receive the Host, of course, but I thought he might
accept a healing. I've only got so much to offer: Good News
again—God loves you, died for you, for sins you haven't
considered yet. . . .

Galt's tough flab stopped my musing. Whoever hired this
one got him straight from TV. He grumbled and spat, since
he couldn't swear, then picked his teeth with a match before
getting out the keys.

Amos was sitting at the head of his bed, back against the
wall. He barely turned to see who Galt was admitting.

"Peace be with you," I said, settling myself in the one
chair.

"That'll be the day," Amos answered.

"So how'd you merit these accommodations?" I asked
him. "I prefer visiting in First Bus."

"Curtis Ballard's told you."

"True, but I'd like to hear your account."

"Long as you understand I'm innocent," he said, turning
to face me. "I been in here three days and you're only the
second person to ask."

He couldn't sit still and tell his story, had to get up and
pace what little floor there was.

It's just another confession, I told myself. Keep your face and voice calm. But we weren't kneeling, and I had no ledge to hold on to. When he came to the part about the notebook, I got mad.

"Have you, then, no modicum of self-control?"

"On paper, for myself, why should I?"

I let that pass. "For God's sake, Amos, tell me what it says."

"I don't read it," he said. "How would I know?"

"You *wrote* it!"

"That's right. Then I let it go."

I just sat there.

"You don't write stuff?" he asked.

"Homilies. Letters, when I have to."

"Don't you ever sort of pour yourself out?"

I shook my head. Then I thought of Saint Paul. "Like a libation?" I asked him.

"What are you getting at?"

"It's Scripture—"

Amos stopped me. "How about you talk out of your own head and I'll talk out of mine?"

"Fair enough," I said. "So tell me what you think you might have written."

"Well, probably . . . it could have been something about her being a female and all." He stopped, his back to the cell door.

"Go on."

"How nothing's happened to her," he said.

"In a carnal way, you mean?"

He gave a belly laugh. "We're good ones to be talking about this—me a hermit and you a priest."

"It won't be funny in court," I told him. "*Is* that what you mean?"

"That and everything!" he said, flashing from a laugh to anger. "I'm not like you, Your Holiness. I can't sort out body and soul and big sins and little and light and dark. It's all together—"

"Then what did you and this girl *do*? Just tell me that."

"I swear I never touched her," he said, and sat back on the bed. "Not, you know, like that."

"But from the notebook, someone might think—"

"Yeah," he admitted.

Give him a trapdoor, Lord, I thought. Otherwise, it's the noose for sure. What I said was, "This is one for Saint Jude. It's a thousand wonders they haven't charged you yet."

Amos put his head in his hands. "Curtis Ballard said writing might not count as evidence."

"That depends on how riled up people get," I said, fiddling with my collar. I do that in tight spots.

"You trying to get loose?" he asked.

"No. Actually, it holds me together."

"Strange, ain't it?" he said. "All them rings."

I looked at him, raised my eyebrows. He went on.

"I used to have one on my finger. You got one around your neck. They're outside of planets, inside of women—"

"Brother, you just don't know when to quit, do you?"

"Truth ain't quit yet," he said.

"That being the case, I think we'd better pray." I closed my eyes. "Almighty God, to whom all hearts are open, all secrets known, be with us in this hour of distress. Give us grace to put our trust in You. If it be Your will, soften the Ingles' hearts that Amos, Your servant, may go free. We ask this in the name of Your most precious Son—"

Amos grabbed my wrist. My eyes flew open, to find his grizzled face close to mine.

"Get one thing straight," he said. "I ain't serving no mutilated boy!"

Given that, I called Galt and left, promising return. Then I petitioned Saint Jude all the way home.

GARLAND: A thousand wonders, the high holy man says. Relax, there's more terrible things could still happen. It's crazy—people smashed, lives tore up forever, and folks say, Well, it's a thousand wonders it wasn't worse than it was. Yeah. The car that killed her kid could have run into her house, blowed up, and burnt it down. Tell me to be thankful. Count my blessings. Buddy, all my fingers and toes is occupied counting the dead.

There's that boy from Travis got hit by a drunk driver. Now I drink—I'm no angel on that score—but the only wheel I ever get behind, the only wheel I got, is the one in First Bus. And First Bus ain't rolled an inch in twenty years. Second Bus don't even have a wheel. I give it to Curtis Ballard for his little boy.

Then there's them boys fooling around in a parking lot down at Calvary Creek. Been to a dance or something. I don't know. Anyway, one of them had a gun. Now I have a gun, too, but I don't take it off my hill and no stranger comes close enough for me to shoot. Them boys started joking, daring one another—one bullet, six chambers, four boys—and goddamn us all if one of them younguns didn't blow his head off. Clyde Napier's boy. Had a scholarship at the university to play ball. Was smart and clean and good to his mammy. And he's as far underground as if he was ninety years old.

79

You going to tell me it's lucky there wasn't two bullets, lucky his mother's heart didn't stop when the preacher brought her the news?

Now this ruin made out of me and Lawanda. You can have your luck. What we've got is grief.

You know why I got to live up on the ridge? Because I don't meet nobody at the corner of my bus. I don't pass nobody in the aisles. No old women bowing to the Lord's will, no men saying his country will be proud.

A thousand wonders. *My* thousand wonders is that, given what we know, any of us goes on.

LAWANDA: Nearly a week had gone by and I hadn't heard from Garland, so I decided to ask Dad what was going on. It was Saturday afternoon right before the football game came on TV. Dad was sitting on the couch with his little kit of polishes, ready to take on every shoe in the house. He had them lined up on the floor like birds on a wire.

"Dad," I started out, "you didn't forget to give Mr. Ballard my letter?"

He looked up but then it was like his eyes backed away.

"No. I didn't forget." He turned a key on the oxblood polish.

"But he didn't give you an answer?"

That wasn't my real question. I knew if Garland had written something I'd have it, but I didn't know what else to ask.

"Lawanda," Dad said, still holding his face toward mine but not looking, "sit down."

I started toward him.

"Not on the couch. I've got my work set up over here."

There was only the ragbag and the shoe-shine box, but I didn't argue. I just sat in the "dump chair" across from him. Noonie calls it that, but we didn't really get it at the dump.

"Okay," I told him.

Dad was so fierce rubbing and rubbing his work boots, you'd think he could warm the hide back to life.

"I wish you had a middle name," he said.

"What?"

"Growing up like you are, you ought to have something new to be called."

He plunged his fist in the other shoe and rubbed and rubbed.

"Ricky calls me Wanda," I offered. Ricky is this guy in band who likes me, I think. He drops his valve oil whenever we talk during breaks.

"That don't help me," he said. "I've got to know who I'm talking to."

"Dad . . ." I was starting to feel weird, the way he was acting.

"Lawanda Jean was what I wanted to name you."

Another time that would have been interesting.

"So what happened to the letter?"

He thunked down one shoe, snapped the oxblood lid shut, and rattled tins till he found the black. Then he said, "I've still got it."

I was mad and confused both. "You said you would give it to him. That's not fair!"

"We're past fair, Lawanda."

"What do you mean?"

"If you'd gone by my word, this wouldn't never have got started."

"What are you talking about?"

"This thing with Amos Garland."

"What 'thing'?" I stood up and went over to the couch. I couldn't help it. "We're just friends. What're you talking about?"

Dad clenched one good black shoe between his knees and took a rag to it.

"I want you to tell me the truth, Lawanda."

82

"I've never told you anything else."

"What were you doing up there?"

"Talking."

"Why would you want to talk to an old man?"

"He's interesting, Dad. He knows about all kinds of things. And First Bus has about a million books and maps in it—"

"I don't want to hear about his bus!" He shook his head and almost groaned. That's when I realized he was worse than mad.

"Why not?"

"Look here, I'm the one asking the questions."

"Okay," I said, my throat hurting like I might cry.

"You didn't do nothing but talk?" He had the black shoes done and was shaking a bottle of sponge-on white. The ball game came on. He got up and turned the sound off. The whole house sort of sank.

"No."

"Well, what in creation did you talk about?"

I tried to think. "School, music, Cardin. We joked a lot." I didn't tell him that sometimes Garland pretended he was a teacher again and I was his student. It would sound dumb, maybe even made up, when it was kind of sweet, really.

"Did he ever hurt you?"

"What?"

"Did he ever touch you?"

The words made me sick, like the time I slammed my hand in the car door, but Dad just went on daubing white on Ray's high-tops.

"Did he?"

"No! That's a filthy thing to say. If I thought up something like that, you'd—"

I was starting to cry now and wiped my sweatshirt sleeve across my nose. Dad handed me a rag, forgetting it was salved with polish.

"Lord God, Lawanda. I don't want to tell you this."

I blew my nose, then tried to wipe the greasy streaks off. "I don't want to hear it either," I told him, "but I've got to, so go on."

"You know them Messer boys got into his bus?"

I nodded.

"I don't reckon they found much worth taking, but they did carry off one of his books."

I didn't know what that meant, but I nodded again anyway.

"One he'd been writing in."

For the first time all afternoon Dad looked at me. There was something he expected me to figure out, but I was mostly amazed.

"I didn't even know he wrote in books."

"I wish you didn't have to. But Galt read some of it when he hauled them boys in—"

"He had no right to do that!"

"He wrote about you, honey." A little coat of pleasure slipped over me before I could stop it, before I could tell myself that Dad meant something bad. "He wrote ugly things, Lawanda. Real ugly."

"What do you mean?"

"About you."

"I don't believe that!"

"Well, it's true." Dad looked away again. "Sex things."

"You can't make me believe that!"

"I'd not have believed it either, Lawanda. I don't want to believe it. That's why you've got to tell me what went on."

"I told you! Nothing!"

"Then we have to show the old man's crazy and clear your name."

"No." I said it plain.

"What?"

84

"He's not crazy!"

"You haven't seen what he wrote," Dad insisted.

"Have you?"

"No, but Galt says—"

"Then you don't know!" I snatched the shoe out of his hands and threw it to the floor. "How can you accuse him when you don't know him? You haven't even read—"

"Galt says—"

"Galt's not God. What's Galt got to do with it?"

All of a sudden Dad grabbed my arms and shook me hard.

"Stop it, Lawanda! You're a kid! You don't know a thing about the world. You got into something you ought never to have touched and you still don't know what it was. I'm your daddy. I'm here to haul you out."

"Garland said how did I know you were my daddy."

He let go my arms. He pulled his hands back, open and empty.

"I'm sorry, I'm sorry." I slid over to hug him and knocked the shoe-shine box off the couch. He smelled so good, like coal dust and dry-cleaning fluid, as well as the polish. The smells were like his arms holding me in.

We sat there. On TV, the red guys were slaughtering the blue ones. I wished I had a helmet like that, and armor. I wished I knew where it was I was trying to go.

HOWARD: I held Lawanda for a few minutes, all the time thinking how fake it was, feeling I could keep Lawanda safe. Whatever had gone on had already happened and I hadn't known about it; whatever was up ahead—well, she'd be on her own soon. I could no more protect Lawanda than I could stop the earth from turning.

When the kids was little, it was June worrying all the time. What if Noonie's rash got infected? What if Lawanda's cough settled in her lungs? It was June who sat up through the night, not able to let go even if they slept like babies. Now it's me. Noonie's clean gone and I've had to accept that. He's nineteen—practically a man, though what kind, I can't tell. Lawanda's an egg that thinks she's a rock—that's what Lawanda is. She can't just go hurling herself into the creek like Noonie and expect to make a right pretty splash.

No sir, I can't protect her from what's happened, but I can sure make Garland pay. If Lawanda won't talk, that notebook will. Let Garland's words speak against him. Then, by God, we can hang him from his own rope.

FROM GARLAND'S NOTEBOOK:

*. . . and I've got all these younguns, children, bodily
U.S. government issue, army-approved. Girls and boys I
kicked once. Do they remember. Weeds in a ditch. I
couldn't lift him. My own boy.*

*Nora all loose-limbed like Lawanda. Those times she
was under me. Nora with a face like anybody's. She didn't
bite. The wind, the kid, the dog. Lawanda hasn't had it
yet. Cool as a refrigerator. Humming. I can't turn the
world around. Couldn't even get him out of the ditch.*

Teeth in the water.

*I got maps of it. A real place where it happened. You
could go back, find the ditch, the tree. Not him. But who
was he, anyway?*

*Some Creation. Look at what we've got: the forked
kind and the pronged kind: push them together and you
got more forked and pronged. And you can love them.
You can love a dog. A rock.*

*Down through the weeds, that's where they are—the
spit of their breath caught like eggs on the grass. What eats
its mate. When the procreation's done.*

*Are you pro-creation? Guess it don't much matter, once
you come down the chute, once your mama grunts you
into this world.*

I like Lawanda's front, don't like her back. I like what she reaches for only I don't want her to get it. Wide shivery mouth, little tits pointed with cold. Shift an old man's gears.

Then pull out and scratch off and fly down the road into dust. Go wherever the rest of them forked things go. Go after Nora. After Chloe and Nancy Catherine. Go on. There's ditches for everybody.

It's a fine line, buddy. It's hotter than whiskey, colder than a froze-up bus. Fine, but we crossed it so far back, we don't remember. Crossed with our helmets on. Way the hell in Germany, way the hell in the wheat field. You ain't seen nothing yet—that ought to be their motto. You ain't done nothing till you pumped in the bullets, bashed in the face till you didn't care, you could drink blood.

Nora bleeding after Eddie was born, bleeding in the floor and me screaming and the light swaying like a goddamn eyeball. No, no, no . . . That's what they do— they bleed. Lawanda does it, right there between her legs. There's a place—I ain't been there in a long time. A ditch. A sharper blood than what you blast out of a man, staining her skirt like wings.

And all the time it keeps happening. When the stars threw down their spears. That's where. Right there. I can put the pin in the map. Pushpin. I can push it into my thumb. But his face won't come back, won't go away. Wound of the world, don't get in my bed. I did it! I did it! You'll have to come get me. Weeds die down. You got to take me alive.

LAWANDA: The only place I could think of to go was to Mamaw—I guess because she sees stuff other people don't. Lucky for me, the next day was Sunday and Mom and I were going over to Little Splinter Creek to make stack cakes.

If you're not from the mountains, you've probably not tasted stack cake—thin layers like white gingerbread, with spiced apples in between. The apples have to be dried, then soaked and cooked and sweetened. Fresh apples don't give it the same taste. It's musty, wintery, like you cooked it in a closet. Geological, too, with the layers. That's the kind of thing Garland would say.

Lucky for me, too, making stack cakes takes a long time— all afternoon, with little pauses while you're actually baking. I planned during these hot times to get Mamaw to myself.

When we got going, though, I realized I hadn't thought this through. Mamaw gives the cakes away for Christmas. That meant we had to make a lot of them. (She stores them in lard cans on the back porch so they don't get moldy while they age.) Because of all the layers, we had to keep washing the pans. Between mixing, greasing and flouring, baking, filling, stacking, and washing, we never left the kitchen. By 4:30, I was getting panicked. There were eight stack cakes cooling on the table and the layers for number nine were in

89

the oven. We were all dusted with flour like we'd come in from snow. Now or never, I said to myself.

"Mamaw," I said into the room, "could I talk to you a minute? It's about Christmas." I hated to straight-out lie, especially on Sunday, but I was desperate.

"I reckon, honey, if Junie can watch them cakes."

"I hate to," Mom said. "We haven't burnt a batch yet, and I hate to be the one to do it."

I wasn't sure if she was kidding or jealous.

"You'll bring them out alive," I said, and patted her on the shoulder. She was wearing a painted-on sweatshirt I'd given her for her birthday. KENTUCKY IS MY LAND, it says on the front. I thought she'd like it and she's worn it a lot. But its softness just makes her seem bonier.

Mamaw and I went into the back bedroom. She had washed her gauzy curtains and one was spread over the ironing board like a veil.

"I made that up, Mamaw, but I've got to talk to you," I said as soon as she shut the door.

She sat on the bed and shifted a stack of curtains. "Set and breathe, Lawanda."

I did. Breathing was hard. The air seemed to catch on the knobs at the bottom of my ribs.

"Do you know why Garland's in jail?" I asked her.

"I know why they say they're a-keeping him."

"Because of the notebook?"

"Yes."

"Do you believe that?"

"I believe they's a notebook and it's got your name in it and it talks about some things people don't like to read, but I can't say if it's what Galt says it is. I don't take the same view of the Devil as him."

"You don't talk much about the Devil." I'd never thought about that before.

"I'm trying to see what's in the light," she said.

90

I wanted to hug her but you don't hug Mamaw. She's like a tree.

"I'm scared of what they will do to him."

"You've got cause."

"What can I do, Mamaw?"

"Pray."

I knew she had to say that, but it wasn't what I came for.

"But *you* don't just pray. You go out and do something. You heal people."

"When they call me."

"Well, I think I'm called."

The winter sun was like a big persimmon. Through the window I could see it slipping behind the mountain.

"Hold up a minute now." She put her hand on my knee. It was as solid and full as Mom's is bony. "Called to do what?"

"When you told me about Amos"—I called him that to remind her that she knew him—"you said you didn't know where his family was. Is there any way to find out?"

"What for?"

"They're what he needs, Mamaw. Not me."

"But do they need him?"

"They'd have to decide that themselves."

"Lawanda, it don't do to play God."

"What about laying your hands on people and making them well?"

"I can't help that. She give me that."

"Well, maybe She gave me this too. I *saw* something before I ever met Garland."

"Saw it in church?"

"No." Mamaw forgets that we don't go to the Pentecostal. You're not supposed to see stuff at the Methodist church.

"It was the first morning I set out to sell magazines. I was tired, almost finished, and stopped to rest. When I put my head down and closed my eyes, I saw Garland. He took my sales folder and turned it into an accordion. And he played wonderful music, like trees and stars and creeks. So I went to see him, though Daddy had told me not to. And that's how this started, Mamaw. The little dream sent me. I'm not saying what it was."

Mamaw took a deep breath. She lifted her apron by the corners, separating it from her dress skirt. Little puffs of flour came out.

"This is steep ground, Lawanda. I've got to pray on it. Just hold your horses till we can talk again."

"When will that be?"

"Wednesday, I have to go to Cardin to the bank. Let me meet you at the schoolhouse."

"What about the bus?"

"Tell Junie we're going shopping and I'll bring you home."

"Mamaw—" Another layer of lying made my stomach hurt. "Are you sure you want to do this?"

She studied me. The room was fading out.

"I'm sure I don't want you doing any more alone."

She got up then and we went back to the kitchen. It was all warm steamy light. "I did it!" Mom said, showing us five layers, all brown and brickle. "Reach me the sugar, Lawanda. This is going to be the sweetest one yet."

MAMAW: I got to think, Mother Jesus.

I got to study. I got to listen to the wind. Maybe when our walls close in, it's just Your big old heart a-beating. Listen. John's snoring in his La-Z-Boy; the stove clock's ticking. Except for them, it'll stay quiet as Jell-O till the 2:00 A.M. train rolls through. Nothing but floors creaking if I walk, water rushing if I fill up the tub.

There don't seem a right move to make and I can't stay still. I promised Lawanda. I promised Lawanda to save Lawanda and I can't. I have got too far up, Sweet Mother. I'm in the air with feathers and no wings.

> O come, Angel Band
> Come and around me stand
> O bear me away on your snow-white wings
> To my immortal home.

Only I can't come home now, You know that. But if I could see You, if I could be lifted up . . . We all need resurrecting, and not just when we die.

Like that long-ago time at the church. Air thick, room swaying. Body not heavy no more. Oh Jesus! Oh Mother, gather me in Your arms!

FROM GARLAND'S NOTEBOOK:

I ain't crazy. I am not crazy. I ain't drunk. I ain't stinking. I am not drunk. I am soper. Sober. *I own my own bus. I own my own body. I'm alive in spite of myself. In spite of whole nations. In spite of acres of craters, headstones. I got a purple heart but not where you can see. Kids, grandkids—your progenitor is still breathing! How come I got no little ones round my knees? 'Cause I kick and trip, 'cause I slap till ears ring. I survived, but the war took my grandkids. Son of a bitch, that's a direct hit.*

This bus is a bigger box than I would have come home in. And I can see out of it. Yes sir. I see the top of trees, not their roots. Worms don't crawl on me unless I'm breaking up the garden. But I can look down this hill and see soldiers moving. And I know what's waiting, hidden below the road.

Left, right, left. Into the foxhole. Left, right—slow it down, buddy. Stay behind the Big One. Big Mother Tank, War, God. In its shadow. Only chance you got. It's wartime, boys. Play ball! Crack them peanuts and pull the pin with your teeth. Got to run with it—all the way down the field—put it in the hole, blow those suckers up! Move it or you're dead on the floor. Come on, don't lay there like some woman. Big old boy. Not dressed for snoozing. Get up! Aw God, head smashed like a watermelon. Come on. Any of you can still get it up, let's go fuck their brains out.

Big party. We're all invited. See the fireworks?

Now class, if the good guys die, it's a mistake. Of course the flags is at home. No drummer boys either. But we've got colors: blood red, shit brown, puke green. Mud, too. Oily water. Drag him by the chin strap. Kick it, little brother. Don't eat it. Might be somebody you know. Ink flows, steady as blood. Wires on the teeth. He died with his braces on. Galvanize him. Look look, take the boot off, take the foot off, take the leg off. If he's ours, gather all the parts. Ship him home. If he's theirs, the Big Boys say, leave him lie. Or do a little more mutilating. Give as good as you got.

Trouble is, I can't tell ours *from* theirs. *Ain't any little boy the same? Flesh, dreams blown open. We keep marching. Robbing the dead for better boots.*

MAMAW: Nora Garland was a Sturgill before she married, so the first thing I did was call her cousin Marylee. I'm not set up to lie, so I just said I'd heard Garland was in jail and that put me in mind of Chloe, which made me wonder where Nora ran off to. This is not peculiar around here. We used to have a column full of that stuff come out every week in the paper.

> Mrs. Al Whitley's nephew, Rob, visited over
> the weekend from Troy, Ohio, where his
> father, Landis Whitley, has been living
> since he left home in 1948.

I didn't know if Marylee would *know*, but if she did, I felt sure she'd get pleasure out of telling.

"Last I heard," Marylee said, "she was running a Kmart somewhere in Louisville—Bardstown Road? That might be right. Somewhere you have to go through a rope of roads to get to."

"So you've been to her house?" I asked.

"No, but B.C. has." B.C.'s Marylee's husband. "He stayed with her a few years back when he went down for that UK–U of L game."

"What's happened to the younguns?"

"They're all growed up, of course. Delbert got into some kind of trouble, but I believe he's in the air force now. I don't know about Ardith. Nancy Catherine's got a flower shop."

"Whereabouts?"

"In the same part, if I've not got my head on wrong. She's a right pretty girl, B.C. says, but she's not married."

"What about Nora?"

"All by her lonesome. Don't think she had the nerve to try another man."

"You reckon she still loves him?" That kind of talk furs my teeth, but I thought Marylee might like it.

"It don't seem possible to me. But the heart's a thorn patch, Ada. One thing I've learned is, you never know, do you?"

"No, you never do."

That's about where we left it, just a few more back-and-forths and I was off. Then I called Louisville information. Nothing for Nora, but there was an N. C. Garland in Beechwood Estates, 43A. Without even reckoning what to say, I dialed. No answer. Of course not—she'd be at work. I got the operator again and asked was there a Garland's Flowers. Sure enough, that dead voice came on: "The number is area five-oh-two–five-five-five–two-five-six-one." I wrote it down, then studied on it. If I called, she was pretty sure to answer. Then what? This was Lawanda's story. I just sat there by the phone, hands sweating. I fanned myself with the phone book. "Exchanges for Cardin," the cover says, "Iona, Calvary Creek." Not Louisville. Not Bardstown. "Mossy Creek. Little Luck." I thought of Jonah and the day Amos asked if I had to haul ass to Nineveh. I thought of Samuel waked up in the night, saying, "Here I am, Lord. Send me."

LAWANDA: Mamaw was standing across the street when I got out of school Wednesday. She didn't smile or wave, just waited for me to find her. In a thick brown coat and with her head tied up, she looked like a bird, feathers ruffed out against the cold. I had the weirdest feeling walking down the steps, like I was something lifted up, about to drop. It just passed over me, like the light in a Xerox machine. Then I was on the sidewalk and headed across the street.

When I got right up to her, Mamaw nodded.

"For a minute, I could have took you for a Ingle," she said.

"Who?" I knew I didn't look like Dad.

"Your aunt Delma Jean, lives off in Michigan."

"I've never seen her." We started walking toward town.

"Made a right pretty woman."

"Where are we going, Mamaw?"

"It depends. I located Nancy Catherine."

"Where?"

"Louisville."

"Will she come?"

"I ain't called her, Lawanda. I figured that was yours to do."

We walked past houses, the library, the undertaker-hardware store. She told me about Marylee Sturgill, about all she'd found out. We came to the courthouse. The jail is a boxy building on the side.

"Let's set a spell," Mamaw said, and pointed to the low wall.

"Don't you want to get coffee or something?" It was cold and I remembered that day I let Mamaw take a chill up at the laurel rock.

"No."

"Garland's in there." I looked at the barred windows.

"I know. I reckon this is as close as you can get."

I had this pain in my throat and made a funny noise. My eyes burned.

"All right," she said. "All right, Lawanda. We're looking to get him out, so drink them tears."

I pushed my tongue against my teeth and nodded. I spread my hands out on my French book.

"You can call Nancy Catherine straight off or you can go see her," Mamaw went on. "I've got money for a ticket."

"Just one?"

"Just one, but it goes both ways. I figure she'll give you a bed and you can come back the next morning. I'll hog-tie your mommy and daddy till then."

"If I call, she might not talk to me," I said, fear drying my mouth. "But if I show up at her door, she'll have to let me in."

"It's her flower shop you got to show up at. You can't leave till in the morning, Lawanda. You got to get there before they even know you're gone."

"Oh." This was a relief and a disappointment. I was ready to go. Then it hit me.

"You know, it's funny I should have to take a bus for Garland."

Mamaw didn't answer.

"Him living in a bus and all."

She laced her fingers together, then twisted them like roots.

"What's wrong?"

"I feel like his eyes is pecking at us. We got to move."

But first, she took a handkerchief out of her coat pocket.

"They's enough money here," she said, "for the big ticket and a bus to Bardstown Road. And calls. Pack you some extra lunch."

I nodded. She reached in her other pocket and pulled out an envelope.

"This has got the addresses and numbers and everything. You call Nancy Catherine when you get in. Don't go another step unless you're sure she's there."

"Okay."

"And if it ain't her, or she's gone to Florida or something, you call and I'll meet you at the next bus back."

"Yes, Mamaw."

"Lawanda—" She looked at me real easy all over like rain. "They's a feather in with them names. It's for you going. It's for Nancy Catherine if she comes back."

Mamaw leaned over and put her cheek against mine. It was skin.

"You're real, Mamaw!" I said, and laughed at sounding so stupid.

"I'm praying on it," she said, and creaked to her feet. When I stood, too, she rested her hand on my shoulder. "I've always suspected the same of you."

FROM GARLAND'S NOTEBOOK:

If I could come back over the bridge now—aw, Hickcock blew the bridge, don't you remember? Last thing he did. Against the sky, everything splattered. Canaan said, "Goddamn! You can pulverize anything!" Said it before we saw Hickcock, his square hands.

I would have sent him back. On the line too long. He'd eaten his peck of dirt, swilled his blood, and then some. Wasn't steady, like he had been. I could see. Them others could see, too, but they weren't looking. And I didn't have the badges to say who lives, who goes forward. If I'd of quit . . . What if I'd said, The hell with this; come on, Canaan, these bastards are going to get theirselves killed; if I'd of just started marching, me and Canaan, seceding from this war, buddy, not firing another round; you boys go on, just excuse us, we done enough murder, think we'll ease on home.

And who would have stopped der Führer then? Damned if I know. But nobody would have stopped Canaan. Maybe not Elias, either. Elias, I threw stones at when he was scared to climb down the tipple. Fool thing! If I'd of hit his hand, he could have let go and fallen. Maybe died. Maybe got a 4-F.

Sack of potatoes, tub of guts. Like I could have picked

*Canaan up and run back with him. Back where? Who
even knew where we were, splayed on the map by some
pin?*

*Round-top trains going by. Bosom of Abraham. So take
the Promised Land and go home. Come on, Canaan, we'll
hotfoot it; we'll swim on back to Kentucky. We'll
discharge our own selves. On the charge of insanity.
Everybody else's. Get you out of this pigsty, take you
home, let Nora fatten you on soup beans, then ship you
back to whoever you call Pa.*

*I've got Lawanda, you know. She's breathing. Doesn't
dream what the world can do. Wants to run smack into it.
You can't tell a person about that bridge. That it's going
to blow. That Hickcock set the charge deep in the
mountain. That the war is everywhere. It's in her
schoolbooks, in the water fountain—turn the handle and it
flashes. All the bones that light up this ground.*

LAWANDA: Here I say I want to go away to college, and just leaving overnight made my hair hurt. Of course, that was different. I didn't know where I was going and nobody was supposed to know I was gone. All I knew was it would take me five hours to get there, so that's how long I had to figure out what to say.

I knew Garland was probably very scary to Nancy Catherine. Maybe all she remembered was him being drunk and mean. So why would she come back to see him? What could I say to her? It's not like I would want him for a dad. But then, I've *got* a dad. And Garland *is* Nancy Catherine's.

I kept thinking how he said he'd lost more than I'd ever heard of. I looked out the window hard, like I could see what he'd lost in the bare brown hills going by. What could he mean except his wife and kids? And his sister, I guess. And whatever the war took. I couldn't do anything about what was lost and gone forever, but Nancy Catherine was just in Louisville. She ought to at least come and look at him. They ought to see each other grown and old.

Anyway, going to look for her was the only thing I knew to do. When you're in trouble, you need family. Plain and simple, Mom would say, though there wasn't a thing plain or simple about this.

I'd brought along this book, *The Prince and the Pauper.*

103

We were supposed to read it for English. Mr. Crawford said it's *so* American, but I didn't see why. I couldn't find any Pilgrims or gangsters. I didn't believe the story, either, but then I wasn't sure I was supposed to. It could be a fable, or one of those other things, an allegory. That's why I like math. Still, I had to read it, and I couldn't think about Nancy Catherine anymore, so I settled in.

There was a guy across the aisle who kept looking at me. He was tall and wore new overalls. He had soft brown hair, thin face, big hands. I kept reading, but his eyes were like the heat lamp in PE. I wished the seat beside me wasn't empty. I wished he would get off at Kildav.

No such luck. But a woman with a baby and another child in diapers got on. I knew he would give them his place.

"You needing this seat?" he asked, bending over me like a willow.

"No."

"Could you move your bundle then?"

"Oh, sure."

He folded himself down carefully. For a minute, the smell of barn and wood smoke canceled out the smell of bus.

He arranged his hands in his lap. "I reckon you can read," he said.

"What?"

"I was watching you with that there book and I figured you could read."

"Well, yes." I didn't know what to say. He did, though. He seemed to have this conversation planned out.

"I was wondering . . . could you tell me what it feels like?"

"To read?"

"Yes'm."

The question made me feel stupid, even though I was the one who could read.

"I don't know. I've never thought about it," I told him.

He just looked at me, his blue eyes fierce and friendly. "I guess it's sort of like singing."

"I can sing," he said.

"And remember the words?"

"Yep."

"You could probably learn to read then."

He nodded. "I never had much schooling. My pa died when I was still in the primer, so I had to quit and work the farm."

"That's a shame," I said.

"Well, I don't know. I took good care of my mommy, helped get my sisters raised."

"I guess that's what's important," I agreed, feeling lucky all at once that none of us ever had to quit school.

"And we've still got the farm," he said, unlacing his hands and resting one across the bib of his overalls.

"How old are you?" It was kind of sudden to say that, but I wanted to know.

"Twenty-six. How about yourself?"

"Fifteen."

"Name's Bev Combs. My pa was Ellis." He held out his hand.

"I'm Lawanda Ingle." We shook hands and smiled.

"Where you going to?"

"Louisville." I decided not to tell him why. "How about you?"

"Just over to Iona to see the man that works on our pump."

We rode quiet awhile. My right shoulder was cold from the window, my left one soaked in his heat.

"My mommy's good," he said, for no reason I could think of.

"Mine, too," I offered. It was true, but I hadn't really thought about it.

"She's broke a bit, though," he went on. "She does her

work around the farm, but she does it slow. She'd understand if I was to get married."

"I'd think so, with you twenty-six years old." I didn't mean to come out hard like that. I was starting to talk like Garland.

Mr. Combs's face changed. It was a plain smooth good face, but all at once it got hard like a fist.

"If you married me," he said, holding one hand open like he might rest it on my knee, "you could teach me to read."

You are going crazy, Lawanda, I thought. This is what you get for trying to sneak out of town on a bus.

"Marry?" My voice slid all over the place.

"We got a furnace in the house now and a gas cookstove. You could bring every book you got."

I studied him. His face relaxed once he'd said his piece. There was a V-shaped scar at the corner of his mouth. I thought about touching it. Then I talked slow to keep my voice even.

"I can't marry you, Mr. Combs. I've got to go to Louisville."

"On your way back?"

"And then I've got to finish high school. But it's very nice of you to ask."

He ducked his head. "Probably they's people ask you that every day of the week."

"No," I said, wanting to give him something. "You're the first one ever."

"Wish I was all it took," he said, and stood up. "You keep on with your books there." Before I could answer, he was swaying toward the back of the bus.

I saw him again a little later when he got off at Iona. He tipped his cap. Lawanda Combs. I waved and felt like crying. We'd only gone fifty miles and I'd almost had another life.

• • •

When I dropped the quarter in the phone at the bus station, something hit the bottom of my stomach. It was a big

106

gob of questions. What are you doing here, Lawanda? What are you going to do if somebody answers? If they don't? If it's Nancy Catherine? If she sounds like—

"Garland's Flowers," a bright voice said.

"Oh God."

"I beg your pardon?"

"I'm sorry. I mean, are you open?"

"Till five this afternoon. May I help you?"

"Are you Nancy Catherine?"

"Miss Garland is at lunch now. If you want to call back after one o'clock—"

"I'll be right there. To see her. I'm coming on the bus."

"Coming from where?" All at once, the voice had a person behind it.

"Oh, I'm already here. Tell her not to worry." Why did I say that?

"May I tell her who called?"

"No. She wouldn't know me."

"Miss?"

"It's all right, really. Don't worry. I've got my own lunch."

I hung up, shaking, but I was laughing too. Everything I'd said was so stupid and I hadn't been able to stop it. I went to get a drink of water and the fountain splatted me in the face. That set me to crying, which was so goofy I had to laugh again, so I lost five minutes in a bathroom stall trying to calm down. You might as well spend some time in there. It costs ten cents to get in.

The ticket man told me how to get the bus to Bardstown Road and I raced to the stop when I saw it pulling up. I was the last one on and the tail of my hair almost got caught in the door. I'd tied it back in the bathroom, thinking I could at least control my hair.

Downtown was all big glass buildings and parking lots. Wind off the river blew dirt in whirls up the street. The ride went fast, past a park, up a ramp, and onto the big road, speeding around with a million other people, then *zoom*, off at a traffic light and the next minute up to a curb.

A woman across the aisle started getting up and I asked her if this was the right place.

" 'Fraid so," she said, tying her head up in a scarf the color of Windex.

"Would you know where the flower shop is?"

"Humph!" she said. "Only flowers I've bought was when my husband died, and the undertaker took care of that."

"Sorry. Thanks anyway."

"Humph!" she said again and pushed on out.

The driver told me I'd been closer to the address when we were downtown. We'd come out around the city and were headed back *in* Bardstown Road. I'm used to a town that you can't miss. He said to stay on three more stops.

• • •

As soon as the bus pulled away, I could see the florist across the street.

It was small: one door and one window. But it looked pretty. The tail of the *G* in Garland looped all around the door glass and there was a Christmas tree with poinsettia lights in the window. Bells rang as I walked in, and there was the scary smell of cold flowers.

A small gray-haired woman stood behind the counter.

"May I help you?"

"I'm the one on the phone," I blurted. "I need to see Nancy Catherine."

"Are you family?"

"No, but she is."

The woman raised her eyebrows at me.

"Send her on back here," a voice said through the wall. "I've got ten minutes to go."

"It's her lunch hour," the woman told me, patting the cash register. I knew I should say I would wait but I couldn't.

"Where is she?"

"Right this way."

You'd think from how she acted that she was showing me through a hotel, but there was only a little hall behind the counter, with a cooler full of flowers on the left and a workroom on the right. When I first looked in, I didn't see anybody, just a pair of tennis shoes upside down on the wall. Then I stepped around a table. Nancy Catherine was standing on her head.

"Hello," I said.

She smiled, I think. It was hard to tell.

"You've got to have more to say than that."

"You talk like your daddy." That's not what I meant to say! She shocked it out of me. My nose burned and I could smell ammonia, like I do right before I cry. Stop it, Lawanda! I said to myself. You're not a baby! Say what you came for. Nancy Catherine's feet swayed like she might turn right side up but she didn't.

"Really?" Her voice had changed. It had a mean sweetness to it.

"I'm from Cardin. I've come here on the bus because I know your daddy. I'm his friend—"

"That must be interesting!"

I tried to look her in the eye to get that sound out of her voice, but it was hard with her head down at my feet. She had on a purple jogging suit too.

"It is. But he's sick. He's in jail, to tell the truth. And I came here because he needs you."

Plain and simple. I was being plain and simple.

Nancy Catherine flipped upright. She was tall and big like Garland. Her face stayed red.

"And who went to get this dad you say I've got when all his kids needed him?"

"Nobody, I guess. You could have tried."

"Yeah, trading scars for a ticket? Who are you?"

"Lawanda Ingle. His . . . neighbor, sort of."

"What's he done now?"

"Well, he drinks and—"

"I know all I need to know about his drinking."

"Do you know you look like him?" The more I looked at her, the more I saw it: if Garland lived better and was younger and a woman, he would look just like her.

"I don't give a goddamn what he looks like."

"Alive or dead?"

"Who are you really? Who sent you here?"

"Nobody. Nobody even knows I came except my mamaw. She bought the ticket."

"Why?"

I hadn't asked myself that; I had to sort through it out loud.

"She's a healer—that's part of it. She knows I care about him. And she knew his sister, your aunt Chloe."

A softer look crossed Nancy Catherine's face.

"I remember Chloe."

What could I say to keep it there?

"She and Mamaw were friends while your daddy was a soldier. Mamaw remembers the store at Redbird."

"I played in that store."

Nancy Catherine's big smart face got prettier as she remembered. Her hair was short and getting gray and capped her head like feathers.

"Mamaw told me about the party when Garland came home," I said, knowing I was headed the wrong way but not knowing where else to go.

Her face clamped down.

"Is that what you call him?"

"He says that's his name, first and last."

"Not Amos? Not Daddy?"

I shook my head for the first question and had to keep shaking. She went on.

"I hid from him that day behind barrels, next to the harness. I can still smell fear in the sawdust and leather, in the lake of pee I left on the floor."

110

"He was mean to you?"

Her head jerked up like she was throwing back long hair.

"Viola," she said to the door, "lunch hour's up. I'll see you tomorrow."

"But, Miss—" said the voice behind me.

"Go on."

The words shoved Viola down the hall and out the door.

Nancy Catherine's eyes took in the room: baskets, vases, ribbon. "You know what this business is about?" she asked me. "It's about hating flowers. It's about wiring the living to the dead."

I nodded. She could have been in a bus.

"And that was my daddy. He loved us the way the knife loves the stem."

"He's grieving over you," I said.

"I doubt that!" she spat out, then ran her hands over her hair. "Come on. I've got to keep store."

She plunged past me. I walked down the hall in her wake. We stood behind the counter while she inspected receipts stuck on a spike post by the cash register. If that was the morning's work, it wasn't much.

"It's Lavonne?" she asked.

"No, Lawanda."

"Well, have a seat, Lawanda."

I climbed onto the wicker stool. She didn't seem so mad now. I thought about taking off my coat.

"Pull off that coat and stay awhile."

I had to say something first.

"Your father is a good man," I told her.

"Like acid is a good drink."

"I ran off to tell you he's good!" I said this louder than I meant to. I could feel my cheeks getting hot. Her eyes were like ice. "He's old and in trouble and I'm part of the trouble he's in."

"You'd better explain yourself."

So I did, as far as I could, starting with the magazines

111

and ending up right where I was. She laughed once—I forget
where—but she wasn't laughing when I finished.

"Jesus, Joseph, and Mary!" she said. "If that's not a case
study."

"It's my life."

"Well, don't think you own it, honey. My life's been in
many a manila folder."

"What do you mean?"

"Social workers, Lawanda. The cleanup crew Uncle Sam
sends in when a disaster like my father strikes."

"He was struck first."

"Huh!" she said. "Do you know what I was doing in
there?" She pointed back to the workroom.

"Standing on your head, it looked like."

"Meditating. Trying to center myself."

I could feel my face go blank.

"Every day at noon, I have Viola come in so I can go
run, and then I meditate. I've been trying to get my life
back for thirty years, Lawanda. What he took. What's in
those folders."

"Maybe you could get it from him," I said.

She snorted. "The dragon may guard the treasure, but I
won't walk through fire to get it. I'm all over scars."

"Mamaw said your mother said that."

"What?"

"About Garland."

She just looked at me.

"When your mother bathed him after the war, she said
he was all over scars."

"Well, he gave what he got," she declared. "And now
he's about to put that map on you."

I didn't want to talk about it anymore.

"His bus is full of maps," I said. "There's probably one
of Bardstown Road."

"Lord God, I hope not."

"He studies things."

"You know he was a teacher?" she asked.

"Yes. Mamaw told me."

"When I was real small, he got a first-grade desk for me and painted it yellow."

I could picture that.

"He got me a big tablet and fat pencils." She looked at the pen in her hand, then put it down like it hurt.

"And you won't do the *least* thing for him? You won't give him one day of your life?"

"You don't know anything about it!" Nancy Catherine's face looked hard, hard. What if she didn't come? It was my fault Garland was locked up, but *I* couldn't get him out.

"I don't know about your childhood," I told her. "But I know about now. I know your daddy's sick and alone, and you look so much alike. If you saw him, it would be like looking in a mirror that showed what could happen to you a long time from now—"

"Stop it!" Nancy Catherine grabbed me by the arm, then let go, horrified. "It's already happened!" she hissed.

That's what I needed. "To *you*, yes," I said, "it's already happened. You don't have to be afraid. But I'm afraid. I didn't know what I was getting into when I went up there. If you won't help Garland, help me!"

I was almost crying. Nancy Catherine looked away. My hands were shaking, my shoulders. I took a deep breath.

"Mamaw sent you a feather," I said. "Will you come back with me?"

Nancy Catherine stared at the cash register. "But La-wanda . . ."

I dug in my pocketbook for the envelope with the feather. "Here," I said, holding out what I figured came from a crow.

" 'Dark as the night that covers me,' " Nancy Catherine said, not reaching for it.

I said, "He's the only daddy you've got."

113

"I know that! And I barely survived him! Why should I go risking my life again?"

"To save him."

"Who says I want to?"

"Because he risked his for you."

"What are you *talking* about?" Nancy Catherine asked, grabbing Mamaw's feather, waving it in my face.

For what seemed like a full minute, I did not know. But I could feel an understanding stuck in my throat. I could hardly breathe. Flowers around a coffin—that's what this place smelled like, a wreath, a garland—That was it!

"In Germany, in the war!" I blurted out. "He risked his life for all of us. He went over there for you and all his kids and family and even me, far down the road." I was saying stuff I didn't know I knew. "And he got wounded—"

"Not much!" she put in.

"Not *that* kind, the kind that tore open his life."

"So?" she said, a little shaky.

"So it never *healed*." I jumped down from the stool and stood there crying, choking through the words. "And you've got to help him." I took her by the arms. "You've got the same scars!"

She put both hands over her face.

I let go and hunted on the counter for Kleenex. When she spoke, she sounded different, like TV.

"That's what my therapist tells me," she said. "Until I face the old man, he's just a roadblock in my life."

"So?"

"So if Viola can work full-time a few days, I'll come," she said. "But it's myself I'm going to set free, not him. He can rot in that jail, for all I care, assuming something already putrid can rot." She ran the feather under her nose, then sneezed.

"Mamaw says the feathers come from angels," I told her.

"Yeah," she said, "the kind that shit on your head."

NANCY CATHERINE: So she comes blazing into my life with a wild tale about my daddy and a mane of hair like the youth of steel wool: Lawanda Ingle—is that a name? Gets me off center, all wobbled into memory, promising to go back with her to Cardin, and then gives me a feather. You know, like from a bird. I don't know what kind. I have enough trouble with flowers. And she says her mamaw uses it in some primitive ritual. You have to admit this is interesting. My daddy's a *nut*, but her grandmother is a *witch*.

She tells about the old woman while I finish out the afternoon. Also she eats her lunch. You would not believe it. A sandwich of something she calls dog meat—they make it from ground-up bologna seasoned with peanut butter and vinegar. She has a hod of this stuff between two pieces of balloon bread. Also she has an RC. I think of my yogurt, rice cakes, miso spread, and sprouts. Of herb tea. Then I think how Lawanda looks new and healthy as all get-out, while I look like what the garbagemen won't take. Well, it's because I ate the equivalent of dog meat when I was her age, that's all. Moon Pies and fatback and soup beans, slabs of commodity cheese. Mother probably put Kool-Aid in my bottle. I know she did in Eddie's. It's what she could afford and it kept him quiet.

I am stunned by this whole thing. I take the feather and
blow on it. The sensation I get is like glitter spilled down
my back. I shake my head. Lawanda watches.

"What's your mamaw's name?"

"Ada Smith. She was a Holcomb."

I laugh. "Holcombs don't mean a thing to me."

There's a frown between her eyebrows, but otherwise she
just gazes. This girl is too calm.

"Does Ms. Smith have visions all the time?"

"No," Lawanda says. "Just that one."

"And it was enough?"

"I guess so. Enough to make her a healer, anyway. That
keeps her busy."

"A lot of sickness in this world."

Lawanda nods. I think how to her that means cancer and
black lung, while to me it means old Amos. AG, his initials
say. *Ag. Gag.* Some dictionaries say Amos means "burden."
Why look it up? I say. Why drive five hours to meet it?

But that's what I'm doing, caught in his ego undertow.
Viola says she can keep store. I close at four and Lawanda
helps me deliver orders on the way home.

"I've done this sometimes with Dad," she offers.

"Yours or mine?"

She takes a deep breath. Maybe she's not all that calm.

"Sorry," I say. "Done what?"

"Delivered stuff. He's the route man for the We-Suit-U
cleaners."

"At least when you get the dry cleaning to the door, they
don't say it's all wilted."

"Sometimes they do," she says. There's a break while she
takes the Pine Cone Supreme to the Haddixes'. "One woman
won't allow her curtains to be put on hangers. I have to
stand in the back of the truck and hold them over my arms."

I hoot and her gray eyes widen as if she never thought
that could be funny. I practice deep breathing till we get
home. Beechwood Estates, and not a tree in sight. Upstairs,

116

end apartment, 43A—small but full of light. And the living room corner is a bay window, faceted out like a lute back. That's where I have my cacti and crystals. Lawanda goes right over to it.

"What a great lookout!"

"Yeah. It's a powerful place for me."

"I have a place like that," she says. "The laurel rock up the hill behind our house. I go there to think."

"You're young," I tell her. "In twenty years, you won't try to think."

"Excuse me?" She turns around, the last winter daylight her aura.

"You'll just be trying to get congruent."

She shakes her head.

"Well, never mind. You want some juice or something before we go?"

"No, but I need to call Mamaw."

"Sure. The phone is on the wall by the microwave." I point her toward the kitchen.

I really want to hear what she says to this woman, but nothing carries.

When I come out with my stuff, she doesn't look so good. She's sitting in the corner of the couch.

"You get her?"

She just nods.

"What did she say?"

"Said my mom pitched a fit even Dad couldn't catch."

"So?"

"The two of them drove all the way to Sexton before Dad persuaded her I'd beat them home."

"Sounds like you're in hot water."

"Boiling."

She smiles a little.

"Let's go then. I expect the longer you're gone, the hotter it will get."

"Can it get any hotter than boiling?"

"It could boil dry," I say, "and ruin the pan."

"Okay."

We head out.

• • •

It's not a bad trip once we make it through the traffic. I like getting out of Louisville, so something besides the river can shape my mind. I just wish it wasn't Amos. I suggest Lawanda look through my tapes.

"Ocean," she says, holding one up. "What does it mean?"

"Just that. Waves, surf, wind, birds. What you'd hear if you were on the beach."

"Wow! Can we listen to it?"

"That's the idea." I snap it into the cassette player and soon we're driving through foothills, earth swell, and the ocean roars in the car.

She's leaning back, her eyes closed.

"You can recline the seat if you want to. There's a handle on the side by the door."

"You don't mind?" she asks. I shake my head. "Wake me up when you need directions."

"Yes ma'am. I wouldn't want to miss the jail."

That's a lie. Anyway, I take Lawanda home first. Her house sits right on the narrow road. Green foundation, white picket porch on a little white box. "Dwelling house," my mother would say, to distinguish it from smokehouse, outhouse, and so on. There's barely room to pull off, so I start to follow Lawanda out the passenger's side, but she is up the steps with two sets of arms around her before I even get my feet on the frozen mud. I'm sliding back toward the driver's seat when I see a big figure come down the steps. Could this be the wild mamaw, bird woman whose feather is in my bag? I get out.

She comes toward me, her left hand hitching stray hair into a bun, her right hand offered.

"You're a good girl, Nancy Catherine," she says. "You've done right to come."

"You must be Lawanda's grandmother."

"Yes, her ma's ma. Ada Smith."

"You knew my aunt?"

"Law, yes."

"And you know my father."

"I'm proud to say I do."

"You're about the only one!" I laugh.

She just pats her dress front. I wonder if she's got feathers in there nesting with those soft eggs.

"He's a man out on a limb," she says, "but I see the tree's yet living." Her nod indicates me.

"Knock on wood?" I ask.

A smile pulls her cheeks into furrows.

"Depends if you're ready to answer the door."

THREE

LAWANDA: I listened to Nancy Catherine pull out, Mamaw labor up the porch steps, Mom rant. Then we went, all knotted up, into the house. Mom and Dad sat on the couch, I sat in the dump chair, and Mamaw took the rocker in the corner. Taking a deep breath, I reached back and flipped the elastic loop to let my hair loose. I was home.

"I apologize for worrying you," I said, "and for going where you told me not to. But I don't think it's wrong. Being friends with Garland, I mean."

"Friends!" Mom said this like a dirty word.

"I don't know what he wrote, but I know he didn't *do* a thing except talk to me. And listen. He took me seriously!"

Dad sucked in his breath. "God Almighty, Lawanda! Serious is just what this is."

"I know that!"

"Then why didn't you come to me? Why did you head off into more danger?"

"Everything is dangerous," I told him.

"Oh, honey," Dad said. "You don't know the half of it."

"I know *my* half, which is more than you know!" I stood up. Anger hit me full force. "You don't know Garland! You don't know what he wrote! Galt could be the sick old man. Did you think of that? How do you know it's not that fat jailer with a dirty mind?"

"Lawanda!" Mom stood up too, her face patchy red. "Watch your tongue! Ray will be back with the rest of the kids any minute. Besides, this is your daddy you're talking to, not somebody on TV. This is the man who keeps a roof and clothes over you and food in your ungrateful mouth."

"Yeah, well, he won't be much longer. I'm not a baby!"

Mom's face drew up. It shut on me like a door. "I'd be ashamed!" she hissed.

"Junie . . ." Dad got to his feet and put his arm around her shoulder. Her hands slashed out.

"No!" she shouted. Dad jumped back. "We'll deal with this. We'll not smooth it over. Lawanda thinks she can go off and do whatever she takes a notion to. Thinks she knows better than us. And it's partly your fault, Mommy. Because you make your own rules . . ."

We all looked at her. I'd about forgot she was there.

"Sit down," she told us.

We sat.

"We don't know about right nor wrong here yet. I prayed and I steered Lawanda, it's true. If that was wrong, I'll repent as soon as we get to it. But right now, what we need is to sit still and see what's going on."

"Okay," I said. "But don't tell us to pray about it."

"Lawanda Ingle!" That was Mom.

"Your heart has to tell you that, Lawanda. And you can't hear your heart for your tongue."

I felt like she'd slapped me.

"Garland's got to pay," Dad said. "And *you*, Lawanda, you who are so all-fired grown-up that you can leave town without a word, you've got to tell us what he's paying for."

"I already *told* you—"

Mamaw cut in. "You won't find the truth by knocking people's teeth out of their heads," she said.

We breathed that in.

"And hate don't heal a thing."

She's got her text, I thought. Here comes the sermon.

But the phone rang.

"You get it, Howard," Mom said. "I'll put on some coffee. My head feels like a dishrag."

"Ngya-hello," Dad said. He answers the phone like a cat. "Who? Oh. Can you hold on a minute?" He snagged the phone cord with his free hand and slipped around the corner to the hall.

Mamaw's eyes caught mine. "Bird on a wire," she said.

"What?"

"Nancy Catherine."

"What about her?"

"That's her on the phone."

Mom came in. She had Hi Ho crackers and Cheez Whiz all laid out on a plate.

"Coffee'll be done in a minute," she said, setting the snacks on the couch. "Eat something, Mommy. You look peaked."

Mamaw took a knifeful of cheese and made a cracker sandwich. "Here, Lawanda," she said, holding it out.

To carry this on, I should have passed the cracker to Mom, but I ate it in two bites. "Thanks," I told Mamaw.

We sat silent except for the crunch of crackers and the drone of Dad's voice. Then the coffeepot made its last gasp. Mom went back to the kitchen.

"Your trip okay?" Mamaw asked.

"I guess so. I found Nancy Catherine, and some man asked me to marry him."

"I forget how far Louisville is," she said, taking off her glasses.

Mom and Dad almost collided, her coming from the kitchen, him through the hall door. When that happens Dad usually says, "Going to have to put a stoplight at this corner." Not tonight.

Mom brought two mugs of coffee. Dad got the rest. We all drink it black.

When everybody was settled Dad announced, "That was Nancy Catherine."

"Don't bring her into this," Mom said.

"I already did," I reminded them.

"You already did a lot of things," Mom snapped.

"What did she want?" I asked.

"*I* want her daddy to stay locked up," Dad put in.

"Children," Mamaw said. "Stop agitating and listen."

But Dad wouldn't. "I've got my rights—"

"And Amos Garland has his," she insisted.

"I've got some too," I told them. "As much as anybody in this. And the first thing I want is to read that notebook."

"Oh no!" Mom said. "I'd not allow that."

"You let me go to school and read the bathroom walls!"

"That's the law, Lawanda. I have to let you go to school."

"Well, it's a law that being accused doesn't mean you did it either."

"Innocent until proved guilty," Mamaw said.

"That's right. We all have to read the notebook and decide what we think."

"And then whatever we want to charge him with . . ." Dad paused.

"It's your word against mine," I told him.

"And I'll tell them not to trust you," he fired back. "*I* can't."

There was silence for a second, as if even the furniture was letting that sink in.

Then Mamaw asked, "Would you *do* that, Howard Ingle?"

"Old woman," he said, "I don't know what I might do."

NANCY CATHERINE: It's well past dark and into high stars when I get to the jail. There's a trio of wise men in lights on the courthouse lawn. All they are is lights, like low constellations. My horoscope. What am I doing here, old man, boozer and beater? Have I come back for more? What could you do to me in jail?

That's what I'm asking myself when I tell Mr. Galt who I am.

"I reckon you got your rights," he says, "but don't look for no reunion."

Amos Garland lies on his side under a blanket. His silhouette is like mountains, folded and faulted. Mr. Galt flips on the light.

"Company!" he hollers. "Are you decent?" Then he adds, "She's come a far piece."

The mountain rolls. "They can't whip you in here," it says. "They just shoot you with light."

I want to announce myself, but there's no name I can call him. The cold boot of my stomach kicks and kicks. He sits up.

"Well, speak, woman! Or are you a ghost?"

"It's Nancy Catherine," I say.

"Nancy . . ."

"Your daughter. You may have forgotten."

127

"You had a big mouth when you was born," he says.

Anger strikes like lightning and lifts my arms.

"Beat up on me real good," he says. "It might make them bastards take pity. At least make them laugh. You know I'm going to court, I reckon. You know I'm to be tried for spoilation of the purest of the pure?"

"Lawanda Ingle came to get me," I tell him.

"Aw God," he moans, doubling over on the bunk.

"She slipped off and came on the bus."

"No, no, honey," he croons, rocking back and forth, like he could put his pain to sleep.

"Are you talking to Lawanda or me?"

He lifts his head. I see what could happen to my face.

"Yeah," he says. "What'd you cut off your hair for?"

"I'm not Lawanda!"

"I mean all that hair you had when you was little."

"Oh."

"It was black, too. What'd you spatter it with paint like that for?"

His words scrape my throat. "I'm thirty-eight years old," I tell him.

"It was so black I used to say coal dust came off on the brush."

"You do remember me."

He strikes a pose, stroking and fluffing his beard.

"Does the Lord remember Moses? Does Moses recall the Promised Land?"

"I don't guess you could quote the Bible without making yourself the Lord."

"Set down, N.C. Pull up that rusty, urinous chair."

I do.

"What's on your mind now? Something your old daddy could help you with?"

I cover my eyes, not because I'm crying, but because I don't want to look at his face.

"I guess I'm here to save your hide," I say, "although I don't know why."

He spits. "Save it, tan it, make you a pocketbook. Or cut it up and braid it for a bullwhip. 'O death, where is thy sting?' "

"Has Ada Smith been preaching to you?"

He looks around. "These walls preach. Even that drain has exhortations, but no matter. I've got Scripture written in my groin."

"That'd be okay if you just wouldn't make other people read it."

He's up so fast, the breath goes out of me, his hands hard on my throat, pulling me to my feet, pushing, twisting the root of my voice.

"Daddy!" I make this pitiful sound.

Then his head butts my shoulder and his hands drop.

"I wouldn't hurt you for the world," he says, stepping back.

"Could have fooled me," I tell him, and then holler for Galt to set me free.

• • •

When I get out, I call the Ingles from a pay phone across from the jail. It doesn't surprise me that I can't talk to Lawanda—they've got to have their scene, too—I just need to make sure I can see her tomorrow. Make sure that she, who got me here, is real. It's bad when your reality check is somebody you never saw till lunch. But there you have it.

Howard says okay, to come by at four. Talks like I'm not worth wasting words on. He's worried about his precious daughter. Imagine a daddy who does *that*.

129

GARLAND: She leaves me, that big hulk of a woman. Leaves me with these hands: what they've let go, what they've throttled. Spitting image. I could have had her around like a mirror all these years.

When Lawanda turned up in my garden I thought I could start all over, thought the rag of her hair had wiped the slate clean. Ah God, you don't look forward, but you look back. I ought to know that. My mind's got slow like a creek close to freezing. Nancy Catherine might have brought me a little something to drink. It's customary when you go visiting.

I got manners. They're somewhere in that bus—behind the canning jars, I think. Now how's a man supposed to can stuff in a bus? Curtis Ballard brought them up there. I forget why. My ma taught me to wipe myself and watch my language, or was it the other way around? Anyway, I been doing it all these years. When I taught down at the high school, I used a music stand for a podium and a nickel ruler for a pointer. I liked to whap on that stand if anybody's eyes drooped or snap the thing on their desk if they went plumb asleep.

Some of them kids was tired, let me tell you. Maybe they slept on the front room floor after everyone else was asleep. Maybe they caught the bus out of their holler at 6:30 of a morning. But still I couldn't let them get dozy. You fall asleep at the mouth of the world and, by Jesus, it will eat you up.

In so many things I have been lost. For this I loved watching Mamaw flap her wings. Old woman, beak on the small-brained head of the Lord. Air in her bones though. You can see it. She may be a turkey buzzard but she can fly.

Is Lawanda like her? She's so new, she ain't hit the ground yet, so there's no way to know if she could take off. And my girl Nancy Catherine? Too heavy, carrying that grudge like a battleship. "Let justice roll down like mighty waters." If it did, would we drown? No justice water backed up in that ditch.

Whoa, there's the question. Let's just step around it like the foul drain in this floor. Or pour lye down it and watch our corruption bubble up.

Lucid, that's what I am, and it's a terrible thing. When you're lucid, the world don't forgive you a breath. You're just weeds growing around the drain, sky tilting above it. I couldn't see how bad it was. There was blood, sure. It's what we washed our hands in. But I told him to buck up, not carry on like that. It was going to be a long war. And him still a peach-face.

I'd heard all about his geode collection, his hometown, his girl. I knew where the shell hit, what tore up inside. But you can't just lay down and die in a ditch of water. You know what I'm saying? He was more than that. I'd told him about my kids in school reciting, "Fourscore and seven years ago . . ." That was a battlefield too. You tell me what this country is but a tale of hope and slaughter. "Every generation has its war." Yeah, and them stripes on the flag, they're cemetery rows; them stars is what they pin on a woman to recollect who nursed at her breast.

He'd promised he wouldn't die on me. And there he was, blood pouring from his mouth. I held him under that water, one of his hands blown clear away.

He was my boy. I don't know. Delbert and my Cardin kids and me somewheres way back. If I could just get him to stop screaming—they was guns going off all around us and still I heard him cry, "Amos, help me!" He knew I was supposed to man my gun and blow some other boy apart.

"Goddamn it, Canaan! Will you shut up?" I shouted, and saw his gray eyes go white. "Son of a bitch!" I grabbed his shoulders. "Stop it! You ain't gonna die!" I shook him, his shoulder bones under my hands hardly thicker than La-wanda's. To get the blood off I put his head under the water, held him there till he calmed down. That made it dark, and all night I held him while they dragged bodies out of that ditch.

He wasn't as big as Nancy Catherine: Indiana's Canaan Zeitz, private first class. A lot of blood in him though. Next morning we was stuck together. They said he was dead. I knew what they meant. We'd spent a night together in the grave and only one of us got out.

NANCY CATHERINE: If I hadn't just come from the jail, I'd think this was the ugliest room in captivity: bile green walls, orange chenille bedspread, yellow rug like a mangy dog. A big petri dish to grow headaches . . .

It's not just my head, though. My heart's like a lockbox. I can hardly sit up for the weight of it. Amos Garland. Old man on my shoulders, all these years between me and the light. That face I've run from, looking everywhere. Here it is in the scabby motel mirror. My father.

I guess this is how you find out the world is round. Run far enough away and you'll come home. Tell that to the Yoga folks.

I'm going to remember. With no therapist, no one to help me. I got coffee from the drive-thru down the road. So old, the creamer turned it green. Polluted waters.

I was born while he was overseas. Early on, I pictured him hovering above the water. Over seas. "And God breathed upon the water," or "brooded," or something. Didn't He? Well, I'll brood over this coffee. See? I can ripple it with my breath.

When I first saw him, he was eight-by-ten, that soldier shot they send you. Good-looking! God and Prince Charming and Santa Claus. The army stripped him of his beard, of course, but Mother showed me old pictures. "Soon as he gets home," she said, "he'll grow it back." My first words could have been "When Daddy comes home": our refrain, our mantra. Whatever came after meant the world would be all right. You can be that young.

I haven't got the patience for this. Yes, I have. I've come this far. I'll just walk into it: Aunt Chloe's store, there at the head of Redbird Creek. Seemed like everything was dark brown except the candy. And this one time, the banner, the streamers. No balloons. Couldn't you get balloons during the war?

A neighbor woman stayed with us while Mother and Aunt Chloe went to meet the bus. I was dancing around like water on a hot skillet. Then the car pulled up. And my childhood ended.

Whoa, there, N.C. Don't get too fancy.

I'd forgotten that he called me N.C. Blocked it out.

What came in the door was not my daddy—it couldn't be! He roared and moaned, tearing down the banner; he lunged against the barrels where I hid.

"I got a new girl!" he bellowed. "Give her here!"

I crawled farther back, squirmed between burlap sacks of rice and beans. Aunt Chloe found me. I had on so many crinolines, my dress wasn't wet, but there was a puddle. She just scooped me up.

"Here she is, Amos," she told him, then whispered, "It's okay. He'll settle down. You got to meet your daddy."

She handed me to a man like the giant in fairy tales—all eyes and tongue and stubble. And he was filthy. I didn't want his breath on me. I screamed and kicked. He held me tight, weaving. Mother pulled me away; fear and grief leaped out.

"You're not my daddy!" I shouted.

She slammed me down and gave me a slap that has turned my head to this day.

He leaned low, rolling his face up close.

"And you're none of mine," he said. "Last thing I need."

Mother pulled him back and took him away. The neighbor changed my pants. I lay down on a couch back near the stove, Aunt Chloe's afghan over me. All afternoon, Mother slapped me under the yarn and the fake daddy spat, "You're none of mine!"

That's how we met.

When I woke up, I wanted it to be a bad dream, but my cheek was sore and I was still in my party dress. After Daddy'd been home awhile, I got used to the feeling. Bad dreams are what you have when you're awake: sleep is the good time. But I could never sleep enough. Fighting or crying would wake me, Daddy throwing things.

After a few months, Mother put a lock on the room that Ardith, Delbert, and I shared. Except for random times when Daddy had a job, she kept us shut up in there. "He does better if he doesn't see you," she said. We would knock to get out if we had to go to the bathroom. Or if she needed to leave, she'd let us use our old potty. We were all way too big for it. She'd put it in the closet to give us some privacy. Also made our clothes stink.

Then Mother got pregnant with Eddie. If she hadn't, I don't know what would have happened. Would they have somehow hung together? I don't know.

Daddy wouldn't let Mother go to the doctor. He'd hardly let her go anywhere by then. He wouldn't have let Delbert and Ardith go to school, but they were gone before he got up. "I'm not trusting you to no doctor," he told her. "They'd as soon cut your leg off as look at you. Besides, I put the critter in there, I can get him out."

Mother had started looking real white and shrunken, even with her belly so big. I was only five years old, but I saw this and it scared me. I don't know if he was beating her then. Sometimes I heard moaning through the wall.

Then one morning after she sent the other kids to the bus,

she told me to get back in my bed and she would get in Delbert's. "We'll pretend it's the hospital," she said. Daddy was in his dead-drunk sleep and I had no idea what she meant. I did what she said, though. In that house, you didn't ask questions.

Most of the morning went by and I got really worried. I didn't smell coffee. If Daddy got up and there wasn't any—

Then I heard him groan, "Nora . . ."

I put my thumb in my mouth.

Springs creaked. He stood, hollering, "Nora!"

I clinched my legs, my toes. He hated to be alone worse than anything. "Daddy," I called, my chin just above the army blanket, "we're in here."

He appeared in the doorway, a wedge. I had my clothes on, could run past him out of the house. But what about Mother? I'd been too scared of him till then to worry about her.

"You females going to laze the day away?" He asked it very easy, walked in slow, and then stripped the covers off Mother's bed.

She was one big belly knot, panting. He jerked her up by the arm.

"Get in your own bed, sister! Don't you foul these babies' sheets!"

She tried to walk, but she staggered, gathered herself low, and rolled onto the floor.

"It's coming," was all she could say.

He nudged her with his foot, that's all, but I jumped him from the bed like a cat. He flung me off and I slammed into the dresser.

"Go, Nancy!" Mother rasped. "Out to the kitchen."

I started.

"No, by God!" Daddy said. "Let her see where this life can get her. Set you right over there, N.C." He gestured toward the bed she'd been in. I went.

Mother caught her breath and then growled. My heart rose in my chest.

"Towels, Amos." The words came in between grunts. "In the chair."

He must have got them under her. My eyes were clinched, trying to force my heart back down.

"Easy, honey," I heard him say, sweet as a lullaby. "Almost."

Sounds came from her like somebody refusing to die. Then there were two cries, a quick shallow one from the baby and Daddy's wail, "No, no, no, no!"

"Amos!" Mother called.

I had to look.

The baby lay in Daddy's bloody hands. He shook it, the little blue and waxy arms flailing. "Blood!" he yelled. "It's all *blood!*"

He dumped the baby on the towels and ran from the room, the house. I sat there, frozen. A blue snake curled from the baby's belly back between my mother's legs.

"Wrap him up, Nancy!" she hissed. "Give him to me!"

I gave her the cold, silent baby, then helped her turn and scoot so her back was against the bed. "Cry!" she pleaded. Then, cradling the baby in her arms, she licked his face like a cat. Still no sound. She laid him in her lap, took his feet in one hand, and lifted him upside down. Hooking her fingers in his throat, she clawed out mucus.

"Wa-a-a-!" the baby protested. "Wa-a-a!"

She looked him over good, then bundled him back up. "You're all right," she crooned. "You're all right."

I watched them. Something in me had lifted loose and was spiraling around the room.

"I need your help," Mother said, her voice pulling me down. "Go to the kitchen and get the matches and a knife. You'll have to stand on a chair, so take your time and be careful."

Was she going to burn him? Cut him? Was she going to kill Daddy? My hands shook with questions.

When I got back, she was nursing the baby and there was a bloody wad of towels beside her. Between it and him ran the blue snake.

"It's all done now," she said. There were tears on her cheeks. "Oh, baby."

It took a minute to realize she meant me. She held out the arm not holding the baby. "Come here."

I put down the knife and matches and let her draw me close. She was so big and damp and cool.

"You want a blanket?" I asked.

"Not yet," she said. "You hold him a minute."

She slipped a finger in the baby's mouth and he wailed at being taken off the breast. Then, with me holding him, she struck a match and ran the flame all along the knife.

"This won't hurt," she said, and snicked the snake in two up close to his belly, leaving just enough to tie a knot.

"What is it?" The words clicked through my teeth. The baby cried hard.

"The birth cord," she explained. "It's what makes belly buttons."

She leaned forward and took the baby from me. I just looked at them.

"Now," she said, "if you could bring a pan of warm water, a washrag, and some towels, I'll clean up this man-child."

It came to me to wonder what we needed with another man. But I just went out to the kitchen. When I came back with the water, Mother said to look in her dresser drawer for a little gown. I did that too. Brought it back on top of the raggedy towels.

I watched her wash him, a little bit at a time, keeping the rest wrapped up. He looked hard at her, like her face was water and he was the thirstiest person in the world.

"One more thing," she said, lifting her eyes to me. "I need the alcohol." I didn't know what she meant. "What I rubbed you with when you had fever."

"The stuff that stings your nose?"

"Yes. It's in the medicine cabinet."

I dragged a chair to the bathroom, but I still wasn't high enough, so I climbed up on the sink. Opening the door was no problem, but when I got hold of the cloudy bottle, my foot slipped and in catching myself I let the alcohol go. It hit the edge of the sink and glass went everywhere.

"Nancy Catherine?"

"I broke it," I said, sobbing. "It's all gone."

There was silence. I got down as carefully as I could. What if I cut myself? What if I bled?

I was just coming out of the bathroom when she called.

"See if there's whiskey left on your father's side of the bed."

I didn't want to go near it, afraid the tangle of covers would writhe up and be him.

"Go on!" she urged.

I crossed the space as if it was a tightrope, then ran with the bottle to Mother. She winced as she took it.

"What a baptizing," was all she said as she poured some on the corner of a towel. "What a father and son," as she daubed around the stub of that blue snake.

LAWANDA: Here I am in American history class. People are giving reports they copied out of encyclopedias. It makes me want to scream. This afternoon I'm supposed to talk to Nancy Catherine. What can I tell her? It's not like I've got anything to hide. The only thing is, it's not quite true to say Garland never touched me. But it's not what they think! It was one time when we were playing school. The bus was his classroom and I was some long-ago student: Miss Florie Adkins, Miss Reba Jarvis. We'd pretend I was there for an after-school conference and he'd go over things: grammar, the Bill of Rights, even poetry. Garland has books for everything.

Well, I didn't mind this. It was weird but kind of interesting to watch Garland turn into somebody else or slide back into who he used to be. But one day when I got there I realized he'd been drinking, and I told him I couldn't stay long.

"But you're here for your lesson."

"Sure."

"It's poetry today."

I felt like when Mom says it's beans for dinner but I just nodded. He walked back to get a book and he fell. Didn't seem to trip over anything, didn't say a word. I called his name and ran back to help him.

His eyes were closed, his mouth lost in his beard.

"Are you all right?"

No answer. I leaned down, put my hands on his shoulders, and shook him. His eyes squinted open.

"You're supposed to be like Sleeping Beauty and give me a kiss."

"You've got it backward," I said, and offered him my hand. "The prince kisses *her.*"

"Naw, it ain't that," he said, waving my hand away and grabbing hold of the seats to pull himself up. "You think I'm ugly."

"I think you're beautiful," I said. The words just fell out of my mouth.

"I'll take my kiss, then," he said, leaning over to plant his lips not on my cheek but on my neck. I felt my face blaze. Garland looked disgusted.

"Aw, Lawanda, ain't you got no boyfriends?"

"Sure. Well, a couple, sort of."

"What're you turning into a tomato for, then? Go on, go on up front and set down."

I did, but I couldn't answer him. It wasn't the kiss I was blushing for. It was that I loved him and I didn't know till then. Not like a boy, like another person. That's why I could see he was beautiful.

We never sit side by side in the bus. For lessons, Garland takes Father Connor's seat behind the driver's, and I sit in Mr. Ballard's. So we're opposite one another and pass the book back and forth.

"Listen," Garland said. "This here's a sonnet."

"What does that mean? I forget."

"Miss Florie, your brains is butter. A sonnet's a schemed poem. Got rhyme in certain places and a beat all through. Studies something. You listen. This is old Willie, number Twenty-nine:

"When, in disgrace with Fortune and men's eyes,
I all alone beweep my outcast state,
And trouble deaf heaven with my bootless cries,
And look upon myself and curse my fate,
Wishing me like to one more rich in hope,
Featured like him, like him with friends possessed,
Desiring this man's art and that man's scope,
With what I most enjoy contented least;
Yet in these thoughts myself almost despising,
Haply I think on thee, and then my state,
Like to the lark at break of day arising
From sullen earth, sings hymns at heaven's gate;
   For thy sweet love rememb'red such wealth
   brings
   That then I scorn to change my state with
   kings."

When teachers at school read poetry, they make it sound like something you could never understand in a million years. The words are all locked together to keep you out. When Garland reads, it sounds like a garden and his voice opens the gate. Old Willie's poem made me sad for that reason, thinking of Garland in disgrace, hating himself. But all I said was, "It's not about you. It says 'bootless,' and you've got boots."

We both stared at his wrinkled work boots, the top layer of leather worn away.

"It don't mean *without boots*. It means *useless*."

"Oh."

"Now do you see how this thing works?"

He handed me the big green book. I tried to read to myself the words he'd read but my eyes kept blurring. Finally a few tears splashed on the page.

"You're a good reader," I said.

"And you're a sorry student, crying on my book!" He grabbed it out of my lap and slapped it shut.

"But—"

"Go on, Lawanda. Get on out of here. I can't look at your ignorant face today."

"But Garland—"

"Time's up. Go!"

My tears were gone and I was mad, but Garland was standing like a thundercloud over me and I didn't want to wait for the storm. I shut my mouth and left. I'd passed the cornfield and was almost to my path when he leaned out of the bus.

"Here's something else from old Willie," he called, waving the book. " 'I had rather live with cheese and garlic in a windmill!' "

"Good-bye, you crazy old man!" I yelled, topping the ridge and starting down. Crazy and mean, too, I thought. Can't stand it that I care about him. And whose fault is that?

Now I see that's a scary question. I'm the one who hiked up that hill.

NANCY CATHERINE: I was suppos-
ed to meet Lawanda at 4:00 P.M., but at 3:30 the motel
phone rang.

"Mom says why don't you come on and talk to me and
then stay for supper," Lawanda said.

"Sure," I said. "I don't eat meat, but—well, never mind."
I was mumbling, trying to come to. "Listen, Lawanda, could
I pick you up and we could come back here or go for a drive
or something? I think we need some privacy."

"Hold on."

Footsteps, voices.

"Mom says it's late, but she'll hold dinner till six-thirty."

"I'll be right there."

"Just blow the horn," Lawanda told me.

• • •

She was on the porch when I got there, and she ran down
the steps, hair flying. She had on old jeans and a black
sweatshirt with the ribbing cut off.

"You look sick," she said, climbing in.

"Sick of my life," I said. "That's why I'm late."

She shivered, looked at her hands lying open in her lap.
"You saw Garland?"

"My daddy? Yes, I did."

144

"How is he?"

We were back out on the road by now, headed the opposite way from the motel.

"Tell me how to get to where he lives," I said. "He wants me to check on his buses."

The lie was automatic, like the door that opens when you step in front of it.

"I can show you," Lawanda offered, "but I don't think I ought to go up there."

"And how am I supposed to know what's changed if I go by myself?"

"I don't know, but Mom and Dad are already—"

"Don't be a fool, Lawanda! You're fifteen years old and he's locked up in jail. If I can go, you can go. I'm in a lot more danger than you."

She just stared at me. We drove on. It was gray, gray—the sky the same color as the pavement, the unpainted outbuildings.

Finally, she spoke. "Turn right at Slusher's Market. That's Hallspoint Road." A pause, then: "What did the lawyer say?"

"I didn't call her."

"Why not?"

"I don't know if I want to get him out."

"*What?*" She whipped around in her seat. I thought she might grab my arm, but she didn't. I took a breath. "That's what you're *here* for. I wouldn't have come to—"

She made me mad.

"You can't control the world. Did you know that? Now settle down and tell me where to turn."

"Around this curve," she said, "there's a school-bus shelter on the right. Pull off beside that."

I did. Behind the shelter was a railroad, behind that the river, and behind that the mountain. Lord have mercy, I thought, and was shocked at myself—or at my mother's voice, still strong in my head.

"They're up there," Lawanda said, pointing across the road. I couldn't see anything but a steep, grassy hill. We got out, crossed the road, and climbed.

Lawanda's a regular mountain goat. She was up at the horizon by the time I'd got myself started on a clear zigzag course. There was no path.

"Slow down!" I shouted, already out of breath. She just ran horizontally along the hill as if standing still hadn't been invented. When I got up even with her, the hill leveled off and I could see the withered garden, the rusty buses. "The old home place," I said, and such a rush of gall came to my mouth that I spat right on the ground.

"Come on," Lawanda said, and stalked ahead, hands jammed in her pockets.

The buses were parked nose-to-tail, with hardly three feet between them.

"That's First Bus," she said, pointing to the older vehicle, the school bus. It was held up by concrete blocks all around, whereas the city bus had two wheels. Lawanda didn't go any closer. I crossed in front of her and stepped up the metal steps.

My mouth went as dry as it had been full before; my heart raced. "I don't believe it," I heard myself say. The only mess was at the back, where the burglars had built their fire. "Did you fix it like this for him?"

"What?"

"Did you make it all neat like this?" The books lined up on the seats, the maps vaulting the walls, the care given to it all I could not comprehend.

"Of course not!" Lawanda was pulling at my arm, dragging my focus toward her. "You think Garland would let me touch his things? You think I was playing house?"

The wind was lashing her hair around and her cheeks were patched red.

"I don't know, Lawanda. I don't know what you were

doing. That's what we were going to talk about." I went past her down the steps and over to Second Bus. Dry grass whisked and rattled.

"Ah!" I heard the satisfaction in my voice as I peered in at the familiar ruin. The setting was new, but the spectacle it held was what my father always created: chaos, dreariness, filth.

"Shut tight," I commented, holding the cold, heavy padlock in my hand. "There's nothing for us to do here. Let's go find a warm place to talk." I was shaking, shaken. Lawanda's face was shut tight too.

"Okay," she said, and took off down the hill.

I looked back a minute before starting after her at the buses backlit by a reddening sky.

LAWANDA: Hiking downhill, I thought about this talk we were headed for. Sex was what Nancy Catherine wanted to know about. It was so stupid. I hardly knew any more about sex than I did when I first got the news.

Mom wouldn't tell me a thing about it. I don't mean when I started growing up; I mean from the get-go, the first time I noticed Noonie had this little thing that went out and hung down where I had this little place folded in. "Why?" I wanted to know.

"Hush, Lawanda," was what Mom said, and that was her last word. I got all my information from Abby Trosper. I asked her my same question, only by this time we were eight years old and I put it different.

"How come boys pee standing up?"

" 'Cause boys are so ornery, they're proud of anything, even peeing."

"I mean, how come they're made different?"

"Oh, Lawanda, you know that."

"I do not."

"You do too. Everybody does."

"Okay, you tell me."

"It's 'cause they have to go to work and pee in strange places where they'd be afraid to sit down."

We both hugged ourselves with giggles out behind the Quonset hut that was Peggy Parsee's third grade.

But I knew Abby knew more than that.

"How come boys go out and we go in?"

"Lawanda, you are filthy-minded. My mama would wash your mouth out with soap."

"I don't care. Tell me."

"I'm not the one to know about such things."

"You do, though. Janie said so. She said to ask you 'cause your mother used to be a nurse."

"Janie thinks she's so smart," Abby said, swirling the brown puddle water with a ribbon that slid off her pig-tail.

"She is," I said.

"Smart is as smart does."

"You mean *pretty*. Pretty is as pretty does."

"It's the same with smart," Abby insisted, her yellow ribbon amber now, her freckles flecks of light. "Janie thinks she's so smart, she's stupid."

"C'mon, Abby. Tell." I knew she was stalling, waiting for Miss Parsee to ring the bell.

"Don't you know where babies come from?" Abby asked, disgusted.

"God?" I asked her. That's what Mamaw said.

Abby laughed and hooted and held her belly and said "God" over and over, choking and sputtering like it was the biggest joke of the world until I grabbed her red-plaid shoulders and shook her hard.

"It's not funny! You tell me right now!"

And she did.

Her flushed face got gray and her blue eyes got cold and she spat out, "He has to put it in you—his thing. Up inside you where the hole is. And that gets babies."

I stared at her. The bell was ringing. She had to be wrong or I would die.

149

Abby looked sick, her little nose and mouth all gummed up on her face.

"You stink, Lawanda Ingle!" she cried. "I hate you!"

· · ·

"Turn the other way at Slusher's Market," I told Nancy Catherine. "There's a Druther's just across the bridge."

For someone so big—maybe because she's so big—Nancy Catherine can look kind of shrunk sometimes. She ran her hand through her cap of hair, trying to fluff herself up, but she didn't speak.

She got coffee, I got a Coke. We sat in a booth by the rest room.

"My digestion is off," said Nancy Catherine.

Shut down? I wondered, like when they turned off our water? I stirred my Coke. I love it when the ice comes right to the top.

I waited. I thought I would just keep waiting, but the weight of those shoulders across the table pulled me to say, "What happened?"

"I've been sunk in the swamp of my childhood."

"Pardon?"

"You can't bring a person back to the present, Lawanda. When you came to get me, when I agreed to come, I was headed right for the past. And it's not pretty."

"Oh."

She stirred sugar in her coffee, took a drink, made a face at it. Then she leaned her forehead on the back of one hand and began pushing spilled sugar around with the other. In a different voice she said, "I want to know why he was so good to you and so rotten to me."

"He was lonely?" I offered.

"He always hated to be alone."

"But that's what he chose."

"Did he ever hit you?"

150

I felt as if *she'd* hit me. "Of course not! Do you think I would have gone back?"

"We did."

I felt cold even though the restaurant was steamy. My daddy would never hit us. The few spankings I'd had came from Mom.

"I'm sorry," I said.

"Did he ever kiss you or push you or touch you?"

I'd been expecting this. I'd thought it through and I didn't want to give my kiss away. It would turn into something else if I said it out loud, if Nancy Catherine heard it. But I was quiet too long.

"Come on, Lawanda. What happened?"

"Once he kissed me, that's all, and it wasn't what you think. We were playing a game."

"Sure."

The slur in her voice made me mad.

"Stop that! You don't know what you're talking about." And I told her about playing school. I even told her about crying on his book.

"And he ran you off?"

"Yes."

"I'm amazed. Listen, Lawanda: you've been up there lighting matches by a powder keg. It's a thousand wonders you're sitting here in one piece."

"You are, too," I said.

"Yeah, but I'm a pretty poor patch-up job."

"Mamaw says it was prayer."

"What?"

"That kept the whole thing from blowing up."

"*Her* prayer?"

"No, Garland's."

"Daddy? Praying?" She gave a fake laugh.

"Not any way you could see. Mamaw says prayer is whatever you do in the direction of God."

151

"I don't even think Amos was *born* in the direction of God."

"That's a hateful thing to say," I snapped, but her face was so full of hurt that I took it back. "Did you know your grandparents?"

"Not the Garlands. His dad was killed in the mine and his mother took to her bed with a bad heart. Died in about six months. I knew my Grandma Sturgill, though. She lived with Uncle Wick: a big woman, had eight kids. Pretty primal."

"And Mr. Sturgill?"

"I think he ran off. I was never sure. You know how it is around here. He could have died out in the field."

"Everybody dies," I told her. "Not just here."

Nancy Catherine studied her coffee. Shivers kept rolling over me like waves.

"It's the things that die and don't get funerals that worry me."

"What?"

A crowd of people had come in all of a sudden. There were fryers going, fans. I could hardly hear.

"When a person dies all over," Nancy Catherine began, "we recognize it and hold a funeral. Likewise, when one person kills another completely. We call that murder. But just die by degrees and nobody notices. Just kill a person in installments and nobody gives a damn."

"How old were you when you left your father?"

"Eight," she said. "And fifty."

"And you've changed since then?"

"I hope so."

"Don't you think he's changed, too?" My eyes were starting to burn. I bit my lip. "I don't know this person you're calling some kind of murderer. The Garland I know is hurt and sometimes angry, but he pulls away too fast to do any harm."

"Hard to believe," she said. "My father never pulled away till he saw you bleed."

"He's an old man," I reminded her, tears like a fist in my throat. "He's not like that now. Maybe he's seen enough."

Nancy Catherine drained her cup. Mine was still full.

"What do you want to happen?" she asked.

"I want him to get out," I said. Tears made me feel stupid. "I want you to love him. I want him to go home."

MAMAW: There's no talking to Howard Ingle. He's got sex in his head and he can't hear a word I say. Some men are like that: it don't matter if it's sex they want or sex they call the Devil's—the world gets shrunk to the fork of somebody's legs.

I went by the We-Suit-U to try to talk to Howard. Didn't want to go to his house on account of June. She's as upset because her man is upset as she is about Lawanda. That worries me. Anyway, Mr. Ballard sent me back to the boiler room, said Howard Ingle couldn't leave what he was doing.

"Who sent *you* here?" was all the howdy I got.

"It's time to ease up, Howard Ingle," I told him. "You got to come back to your human self."

"Mamaw," he gritted out, like he was holding his temper with his teeth, "this is something you don't know nothing about."

"You think I got my children by holding hands?"

"Good God Almighty!" He wiped his face. He was sweat-slick where he wasn't dusted with soot. "Just take your feathers and your filthy mind and go home."

"It's not filthy! That's what I'm here to tell you. Man and woman: it's as clean as the ground."

He hauled off and spat a big gob at my feet. "You think Lawanda and that old man—"

154

"No, I don't, son, that's what I'm trying to tell you. He never laid a hand on her. I was up there—"

"Once!" He looked at me quick. He was watching dials.

"And I know what I saw, what it was like."

"Then why are you talking about sex?"

"Because that's what you're thinking! And you believe the whole thing's filthy—"

"Goddamn it!" He was getting up more pressure than the boiler.

"You do. You'll call it something pretty for you and June, but anything not locked up in a house, you call filthy. That's why you can't stand to think—"

"Mamaw!" He jammed a shovel in the coal pile. "Get out of here!"

"I'm a-going, but just—"

"Now!" He raised the shovel and shook it at me. I let myself out the back way.

• • •

So what could I do but go try Garland? Muddier waters but at least he's a deeper pond. Galt shook his head at me.

"He won't take to no preaching."

"It ain't Sunday," I said.

"With women preachers, I hear that don't make much difference."

I looked at his face, a dough ball that needed punching down. "Lead the way," I told him.

Garland looked up at me from his cot. He was scary white, limp.

"Look what the cat drug in," he greeted me. "Ada—Lawanda's mamaw—Smith."

"At least I ain't a dead rat," I answered.

"Me neither. Yet."

"Then let's try to reckon some stuff while we're alive."

155

"Whoa, there, Feathers. Don't judgment come when you're cold?"

"I didn't say judgment."

He pointed to the chair. I pulled it closer to his cot and sat down.

"If you can come here, I guess I can listen. Watch your tongue, though. They's lawyers bugging the walls."

"Let them listen. Nobody's heard the truth yet."

"About what?"

"About you and my grandbaby. Has anybody asked you?"

He leaned back against the wall, closed his eyes, and sighed.

"Not a soul," he said.

"Ain't that crazy?"

He opened his eyes just a squint. "I don't know, Mamaw. Stay in here a while and you can't tell beans from farts."

"You know who Howard Ingle is?"

"Yes."

"Well, he's hopping around like a flea because of this thing Galt said you wrote."

"It's a notebook. Diarylike thing."

"Whatever it says about Lawanda, Howard Ingle thinks you done."

"I'd like to get a really sharp pen and slit Galt's throat."

"He don't bleed ink," I reminded him.

Amos sat straight up. "What's that supposed to mean?"

"I figure you're a person who don't like blood." This was a thing I just knew.

He stood up and clenched his fists, then walked over to the bars. "Go on."

"What happened, Amos?"

"I was as good to Lawanda, respectful, as I would be of my own daughter." He laughed. The sound hurt. "No, by God! I was better. Ask Nancy Catherine. I never hurt

Lawanda. Ran her off a couple of times. That's all."

"And that writing—"

"That's my own goddamn business! It's me, *inside*, not something out in the world. How would you like it, Mamaw"—he leaned over and took hold of my dress front—"if somebody tore the prayers out of your mouth and printed them up in the paper?" He pulled me closer, his forehead almost on mine. "And then accused you of wanting the wrong thing, or too much, of being a sick old woman?"

I put a hand up to touch his shoulder and he let go. The front of my dress was twisted sideways. I reached in for what I'd brought.

"You're a sight," he said.

I gave him the speckled feather.

"If they yank out my prayers today, they'll find your name."

NANCY CATHERINE: "Okay, Lawanda," I said, "I hear you. And for all the hurt the old man inflicted on his own kids, it never was sexual. I'm not sure that proves anything for you, but . . ."

She nodded, blew her nose in her napkin. I changed the subject.

"We'd better head for that dinner. What do you suppose your mom will fix?"

"Meat loaf," said Lawanda as we went out the door. "Turnip greens," as she went around the car. "Mashed potatoes," as she climbed in. "Combination salad," as she settled herself. "Pineapple upside-down cake," as she leaned forward, lifting her hair and fanning it out over the back of the seat.

"Sounds like you read it off a menu," I told her.

"I did. It's on the front of the refrigerator."

"Every day?" This was amazing.

"A week at a time. Mom says if it's not up there, she worries all day about what she's going to feed us."

"And it doesn't change when you have company?" I was curious.

"We added the cake," she said.

"Oh."

We were quiet then till we got to Lawanda's house. Her dad met us at the door.

"You better be getting in here, girl," he said to his daughter, clapping her on the shoulder. Then he looked at me. "Come in, now. Make yourself at home."

"Please call me Nancy Catherine," I said.

"All right. I'm Howard and June's—"

"Come on in," June called from the kitchen. "It's on the table."

The room was at once crowded and pinched with neatness. Lawanda got to work settling Jeff while her mother sliced the meat loaf. She stopped long enough to say hello and direct me to my chair with the knife.

The meat loaf looked good enough, if you like dead cows.

"I'm afraid I don't eat meat," I said.

"Oh, dear—" June started.

"No, I'll be fine, really. I just don't want you to think I don't like what you fixed."

"Do you?" Dessie asked. She had straight crow black hair and a smart-alecky look on her face.

"Dessie!" Howard Ingle sounded disappointed. "Watch your manners!"

"I don't know," I said. "It's been so long since I ate meat loaf."

At this point, the conversation was interrupted by the back door opening. A big lanky boy loped in.

"Wash up, Ray. You're late," June told him.

"Practice," he said.

"Early basketball," Lawanda told me.

In a minute, he was back and we all sat at the table while Howard said a graceless grace. Then came plate passing and polite conversation. June was working hard to hold my interest, Howard to hold his temper. This didn't seem to faze Lawanda. Me, it about did in. Finally, I took the plunge.

"I don't know how to get us out of this mess my daddy's got us in," I told them.

"Lawanda here got *you* in it," Howard pointed out.

159

"True enough, but I don't regret that." Was I lying? "I needed to come back," I said, "and I would have never done it on my own."

June nodded. Lawanda pushed her potatoes an inch farther from her untouched meat loaf. Maybe this was getting to her after all.

"We should get Garland out," Lawanda said, "and then you can go home."

"Hush!" Howard ordered.

This startled Jeff and he turned over his milk. Lawanda jumped up.

"Wait till the children are done, Howard," June advised. "I'll send them on the porch with their cake."

Ray inhaled his food, Dessie sulked, and Jeff dawdled, but finally they were gone.

"Lord have mercy," June said.

"What's that for?" Howard wanted to know.

"You blessed the food," June said. "I reckon I can bless the talk."

They looked at each other.

"Fair enough," he agreed.

"What I understand from talking with Mr. Galt," I began, "is that my father is officially being held for public intoxication and resisting arrest and that bond will be set when the court meets Monday. What they're really keeping him for, though, is to give you time to work up a case against him regarding Lawanda."

"What?" Lawanda's body rose with her voice, both lifted in astonishment.

"That's true and you knew it," her daddy said. "I told you myself. Now sit down."

"Do you have a lawyer working on it?" I asked.

They all stared at me. Finally, Howard spoke.

"That'd be the sheriff's business, wouldn't it?"

"Not until you bring charges. And to do that, you have to have testimony—"

"We got that notebook!" Howard pounded the table.

"I'm not sure," I told him, "but I don't think that's admissible evidence."

"Your lawyer tell you that?"

"I didn't call one."

"Why not?"

"Because she's not sure she wants Garland out," Lawanda broke in.

"Partly," I admitted. "But also I'd have to *find* a lawyer."

"I thought every soul in Louisville had a lawyer," June said.

"Well, they don't."

"Wait a minute!" Howard said, turning to me. "Why don't you want him out? He's your own daddy."

"That's why," I said. "I'm scared of him."

"See!" His arm shot out, finger pointed, as if to poke into the eye of what I'd said. "A grown woman, his own flesh, who don't even live here, is scared of him. That's why we got to keep him locked up."

"She's scared of the *past*," Lawanda spat out. "Something that already happened! And I don't know what you're scared of. Me, I'm scared Garland's going to die locked up where you wouldn't keep a dog!" And she got up and walked out the back door.

I started to follow.

"Leave her be," June said. "She needs to cool off."

I turned around. Even as I did it, pivoting on the scrubbed linoleum, I could feel a larger turning.

"She's right," I told them. "I *am* scared of the past, what's over. That man I saw last night wasn't my daddy that hurt me—"

"He's your daddy that hurt Lawanda!" Howard grabbed my arm.

"He's what became of my daddy," I finished, turning my wrist till he let go.

"Lawanda doesn't *act* hurt," June put in. "There's no

161

sign of anything bad, except all this upset." She turned to Howard. "I don't see why you can't just let it go. Mommy said you wouldn't even talk to her today." Howard raised his palm to stop her, but she ignored him. "And you know what she did then? Went to see Garland. Said he looked bad."

"Your mommy has no more sense than Lawanda!" Howard snapped at her. "Do you think I care how the old man looks?"

"Well, I do." What? What was I saying?

"Me, too," Lawanda said. None of us had heard her come in. "And if the bond is set Monday, I'll bet Mr. Ballard will pay it and get him out. Unless *you* talk him out of it." She glared at her father.

"Don't know as I can," Howard said. "He's blind as you."

"Or can see as deep," I told him.

"Does that mean you won't help me?" he asked.

"Help you what?"

"Keep your daddy where he belongs."

I took a deep breath, looked from Howard to Lawanda, thought of the distance between Amos and me. *You're not my daddy!*—the first thing I ever said to him. But he was. Now and ever shall be.

"If you mean in jail," I said, "no, I guess not."

He got up from the table and walked away.

LAWANDA: I stormed out the back door and stared at our steep patch of yard. That's my life, I thought. Open a door and walk into a mountain.

It was cold and I didn't have a coat and I was glad. I wanted to get numb. I wanted to freeze all the questions: Nancy Catherine's, Dad's, mine. Was I in love with Garland? Stupid idea. But how would I know? It's not like I'd been in love with anybody else. Didn't my heart beat faster on the way to see him? Yes, but it was a hard climb up the ridge. Didn't I want him to hold me? Not that I knew of. I mean really, I had never thought about it. Yeah, but now that I had . . . Maybe. I guess. I don't know.

But he didn't. That's the point. So what if he felt that way about me? You can feel anything. Is that bad?

They're talking about action, I told myself, circling the coal shed, picking up a good-sized chunk. *Innocent in action*, that's what I'll say. This piece of coal could have been a diamond, given enough pressure, enough time. Or it could have been burned to cinders in the grate. But none of that happened. They were reading *action* where Garland wrote *feeling*. But there wasn't any action! For that matter, they didn't even know what he wrote.

What *did* happen between Garland and me? I went over it. We were friends. I needed someone to talk to and I could

163

talk to him. What's wrong with that? Nothing. Okay, why was I scared, then? His drinking. That's it? No, there was something *there* when he was drinking, something threatening to get out—

But it didn't. I would say that if I had to.

I went back into the overheated house—still mad, but clearer. They could accuse all they wanted, but I knew what I knew.

HOWARD: They're going to let that man out, by God. Lawanda won't say what he done, and what he wrote won't hold him. I've tried to talk to Curtis Ballard, get him to promise not to go bond, but it's like his eyes are sealed, his ear flaps sewed over. "Good at heart," Mr. Ballard says. "Whatever Garland may have written, I know he's good at heart." I thought a man showed himself by his work. "By their fruits ye shall know them." A good heart ain't enough! Even if he has one, which I doubt.

You know something else? I don't think Mr. Ballard wants to be wrong. Garland's like some strip-mine bench he thinks he's reclaimed. See? It'll grow kudzu, poison ivy, stinkweed, bindweed, beggar-lice. He can't admit that a garden plant won't last in it till the fruit sets. Sour ground, I'm telling you. Sowed with salt.

Lawanda's a wild plant anyway. Too much like her mamaw. Thinks she can do anything, go anywhere she pleases. If she was a boy, now . . . What I don't get is how Mamaw raised Junie, a regular woman, a person with sense. Whatever Mamaw's got loose in her skipped straight to Lawanda. I should have seen it coming. I remember the time Lawanda climbed up on top of the shed. I'd come out to the coal pile and saw her tottering up there, not about to admit she was scared. Before I could say a word she hollered, "You let Noonie play up here!"

"He's older. Now come on down."

"He's a boy, you mean."

"Now, Lawanda—"

" 'Boys will be boys,' Mom's always saying. What about girls?"

"Girls will be switched if they don't mind their daddies," I said.

She climbed down.

"I told you never to set foot on that ladder."

"God said I could," she taunted.

"You leave God out of this!" I took a forsythia sprout then and there and welted her legs.

Fat lot of good that did. She didn't need God's go-ahead to climb that hill. All she needed was the notion. All the seed needs is a little wind to ride out on and it can land in a garden or a tar pit. Well, I've dug up the plant. It's wilted but surviving. Now I got to take care of that tar.

NANCY CATHERINE: When I left the Ingles', I went back to the motel, thinking to settle in for the night. I couldn't do it. I'd seen too much: the buses, Howard's blindness, that I was on Lawanda's side. I couldn't lie down with a shrieking orange carpet and *that*.

So it occurred to me to take another hike up Cade's Hill. I thought if I could fix First Bus in my mind—its order, the care Amos gave it—I'd have something else to hold against all I knew of him, something to add to Lawanda's account. She found him in his garden, not his wilderness; they met in his library.

So, getting my jacket and making sure the car flashlight worked, I drove off. It seemed much farther to Hallspoint Road in the dark, without Lawanda. I was tempted to turn around at each traffic light. What I was doing made no sense. Where I was made no sense. How could somebody I'd never met suck me back into my father's life? Back where I swore I'd never be?

Even with the bypass opening up one side of the town, Cardin is a jail in itself, walled in by mountains, choked by the river, barbed wired by the railroad. I looked at the rim of ridges, a green-black worse than dark. I looked at the sky above, constellations punched through like the design in God's pie safe.

Mamaw, I thought. That's the Mamaw channel coming through. Lawanda's got me wired up to all these people. She's a connector. And it hit me: she could be my daughter. I'm old enough. She could be Daddy's granddaughter. But he doesn't have any. Four kids and not a single grandchild.

Lost them in the war.

It was more like a sign I passed than a thought. What channel was that?

The school-bus shelter was hard to see in the dark, so I almost passed it and was going too fast as I got off the road. I skidded in the gravel and came close to losing control of the car. My heart was hammering when I started across the road.

Funny, in Louisville I wouldn't think of walking through an empty lot at night, wouldn't jog in Cherokee Park or even walk back to my car after a movie by myself. But here I didn't hesitate. Maybe my obsession made me feel safe. I headed up through the weeds, the flashlight beam zigzagging ahead of me. I was relieved to be doing something.

But when I reached the top of the ridge where the buses sat, I shivered. There was a charge in the air, like an odor, except I felt instead of smelled it.

My first thought was that the burglars had come back, and I ran to First Bus, meaning to scare them off. I climbed the steps and peered in, but I could see neither light nor movement.

I walked to the door of Second Bus. Nothing going on in there, either. Still the feeling persisted. Bad vibrations. I sat on the steps to think. Was it just memory warning me away? Or maybe it was little Nancy Catherine looking at me from her trapped space, saying, You can escape! Forget about me! Go!

I was listening for her, but what I heard were footsteps. Without thinking, I turned off the light. Then I saw him, enlarged by his coat and the darkness, like a shadow thrown against a wall. He was carrying a gas can. His face wasn't even covered. He came closer, set the can down, and began working off the lid. He didn't see me or seem to sense anyone close by.

I couldn't let him go any further. I flashed the light in his face.

"Howard Ingle," I said, "you don't want to do that."

He jumped, then froze, the smell of gas sloshing out of the can. I couldn't see his face, so I went on. "You have no right to damage my father's property, and you'll wind up further back in jail than he is if you do."

"What about the damage he's done to *my* property?" Howard asked.

"Your daughter's not property," I told him. "And you have no proof of damage."

"I got a gas can," he said. "Sometimes you got to burn the field clean."

Fear pricked my spine. I was going to have to stop him.

"This is a person's house," I told him. "Not a field."

"Some house!" he said, disgusted. "Some person." And he started around the bus, tilting the can. "Go home, Nancy Catherine," he called, "and you won't have to see this. Not a soul will know who did it."

When he heard me get up, he began running, splashing the gas against the bus. But I heard something else. I swung the light behind me. It was Lawanda! Oh my God! She ran past me, yelling, "Daddy! Stop it! Stop!"

Before she could reach him, something sparked in his hand. She jumped on his back and they both fell as a fuse of fire ran around the bus.

"Goddamn you, Howard!" I screamed, pulling Lawanda from his back. Then I tore my jacket off and began beating at the flames. Howard just stood there. I was working my way around the bus, knowing it was useless, when I saw Lawanda go for the gas can. I hollered, "No! No!" but she raised her foot to kick it into the garden. Fire got there first and there was this *boom*, and it looked like a starburst. For a minute, I couldn't see Lawanda, then she appeared, robed in flame, the corn patch behind her.

"Howard!" My voice spiraled. I ran toward Lawanda and he was there.

HOWARD: I could see the maps on the ceiling start to curl. But then something blew up like God Almighty and I was running and it was Lawanda, Lawanda burning, which couldn't be, and I jerked off my coat and she was already on the ground, rolling. I threw it over her, her hair. I beat on her, lay on her, smothered the fire out. Then I had to drag her away from the flame that was coming. Her face was black, her eyes still as the moon. I carried her down the hill, Nancy Catherine screaming all the way.

She took us to the hospital. Lawanda's so big, it was hard to put her in the car. I couldn't get in the backseat with her. Nancy Catherine said she was breathing okay, to stop moaning, and I said would she take me to jail after the hospital. She said I was burned, too, we all were, and I started this crazy crying. "Listen for your daughter!" she said. "Shut up and listen!"

FOUR

MAMAW: Mother Jesus, let Your eyes be the headlights pulling me across this mountain. I've driven many a night but it's never been this black. "Not Lawanda," is the only prayer I got in me, and that's no good. It *is* Lawanda. Already is. I'm the one says you don't want sacrifice, and here's my own grandbaby . . . She's got to live, You hear me? We ain't got room in our pain to lose Lawanda.

What did *she* do, anyway? The least of anybody. Amos, Howard, me, even Nancy Catherine, but *Lawanda*? Ain't You paying attention? This is wrong, the wrong way around—

Lordy mercy, I've got to slow down some. I just about missed that curve. The crack in the windshield don't help, either. Coal truck kicked up a rock last week. Window down and I could have been blind, dead over Pine Mountain.

> Deep calls to deep
>   at the thunder of your cataracts;
> all your waves and billows
>   have gone over me.

Waves and billows of fire.
Just passed the turn to Stony Fork. We've had many a

175

picnic there. Frying apples over a woodfire, bees buzzing. And Lawanda running with a gang of ragtag kids. Dessie getting stung. Where can we go, Mother Jesus, if we lose Lawanda? Will You come wake her up like Lazarus? Give her a new skin?

June on the phone was pure heartbroke. On top of everything, Ray's saying he won't see his daddy again. Between her man, the other younguns, and Lawanda, where's she supposed to go? It's like the old hymn says:

> Where could I go,
> Where could I go
> Seeking a refuge for my soul?
> Needing a friend
> To help me in the end,
> Where could I go but to the Lord?

Your love is the one road we got, Mother Jesus. Without You, it's the rock wall or the cliff. Sometimes the fog's so thick you can't see no edges. Like now. So reel us in. Reel us close and heal Lawanda. Give us forgiveness, Howard most of all. Give us healing. You, who stood the fire of all our hate. Amen.

NANCY CATHERINE: I got Lawanda and Howard to the hospital, called June and went to pick her up, then drove to the jail. I had a few singed places, but nothing that wouldn't keep, and anyway, it was my heart that hurt. I wanted that notebook so I could read and judge for myself, and then I wanted my daddy out of that jail. I wanted everybody at the hospital, where we could keep watch for Lawanda and see we all cared about the same thing.

I'd already been considering how to get the notebook; this holocaust just gave me a trump card to play. It was about one in the morning when I got to the jail, so I had to buzz Galt on the intercom. He has an apartment on the premises.

"I'll be down in a minute," he said, sounding none too happy about it.

I didn't care. "Mr. Galt," I began, before he even sat down in his office, "do you know what happened tonight?"

He looked blank.

"About the fire?"

He shook his head. So I told him, bluntly and bitterly. "Good God!" was all he said.

I set in. "Because you've been holding my father here in hopes of more serious charges—"

He spluttered in protest, but I plunged on. "I know about the notebook and how you slandered my father based on evidence illegally seized."

He raised his hands. I pressed hard: "And since, if you had not been holding him here, Howard Ingle would not have burned the buses, nor Lawanda been a victim of the blaze, I propose that you give me my father's notebook with the understanding that this will be the last we hear of either matter—my father's writing or your manipulations—and that, as soon as I find a place for him, you'll release him upon payment of the bond."

"Well, now, Miss—"

"Ms."

"Ms. Garland, I don't even know if I can remember all—"

"You don't have to. I'll write it down. You can make a copy and we'll both sign."

"But I don't think I did anything wrong."

"I don't think my father did either."

He shifted papers on his desk, whistling low through his teeth.

I laid down my high card.

"There's a girl in the hospital in critical condition because you tried to play God."

His head jerked up.

"Well, I reckon, Miss—"

"Ms."

"Garland, as a favor to you . . ."

I wanted to say, It's no favor to me if you save your skin, but I held my tongue. The object wasn't to have the last word, but to have the notebook and a clean way out.

He handed a legal pad across the desk and I wrote out the agreement. The paper was a sick green. Like I felt. But when I finished, he made the copy on the office Xerox and we both put our names to it.

I was shaking as I walked back to the car. I tried to

concentrate on avoiding bird shit and tobacco splats on the sidewalk. I thought the courthouse square was deserted, but I turned and saw a one-legged man sitting at the foot of the doughboy. His twisted face followed me all the way to Druther's. Was he mangled by the war that blew apart my family? Did the notebook hold a face more pitiful than his?

LAWANDA: One nurse is hunting with a needle under my collarbone. Another nurse is cutting my clothes off and I'm ashamed. Charred skin comes off with the T-shirt, the long strips of jeans. I look for the pink-white surface that was me. All that's left is the folded-in skin between my legs, flashing when they move me.

I'm searching for pain, too, but I don't feel any. Mom looks like she's going to die, and the policeman who came to file a report couldn't hide his horror. If you can't do better than that, you need a different job, I wanted to say. But I'm too polite, and besides, my voice is missing. There's just a squeaky sound.

Everybody's talking about fluids and hooking me up and monitoring, but they also have to peel off what will come off. My hands you would not know are hands. I think about playing the tuba, learning to type. I wonder where tears come from.

The nurse tells Mom to leave. They've got to do some cutting. Mom asks if she could touch me somewhere. Only if she scrubs. Then she can touch my head, which isn't burned. This is good. I feel like a guy on a space walk who's just been tethered. Hold fast, Mom. Call Mamaw.

I try to squeak this out. She says she did, I think, and

then says good-bye, her white face like the moon. Stay in orbit now. Don't leave me.

They want to know if I can feel anything in my foot, in my groin. I shake my head. They want to know why I'm awake.

I wish I could sleep. I wish they'd turn off the lights and go away, not touch me, except Mom, and Mamaw when she comes. I want to go away myself. I can come back later, if I have to, when I've had some sleep.

But there are more faces above me all the time—masked now, their eyes anxious, their words puffing the cloth.

I guess I could be going to die. This thought's like a bird. It lands and lifts off. But I'm not wanting to go. I just got here.

Then I think, If I die today, I'll have to do something else tomorrow. What would that be? And where is my dad?

There's a lurch and the ceiling starts to move. Somebody tell me where I'm going. Bags of fluid sway above me. I see the wrist of the guy who's pulling me, perfect paper white skin. Write me a note, somebody, if you're not going to speak to me. My name is Lawanda.

"Got a bad one here," somebody says. I hear a low whistle. "A lot of third-degree."

"Jesus Christ!" comes the reply.

It's Mother Jesus, I want to say. You can take it up with Mamaw.

And just as we come to a stop, her face appears, right over mine. I can smell her breath. She puts her hand on my head, steadying. Somebody jerks it away.

"Lawanda," she says. "Precious child of God."

It's the first time I've ever seen her cry.

NANCY CATHERINE: At Druther's,

I was afraid to open the object in question. "Mead Paper," it said on the front, and I thought of honeyed wine as I drank Styrofoam coffee and stared at the plastic orange bench. I also thought of Pandora's box. If I opened this, who knew what would fly out? I might agree with Galt. Then what? But I had to do it. You don't get to choose your parents. My therapist said that. You don't get to choose your scars or where your heart breaks. Lawanda didn't choose the fire. Daddy didn't either, I realized, my brain going orange, my ears filled with sizzle. Daddy didn't get to choose.

I turned to the pages Galt had marked with a matchbook cover. All about weeds and the army, a ditch and Mother and some boy. There was sex; there was blood—war blood, menstrual blood—but it was all mixed up with this place, this boy: "I couldn't lift him. . . . You could go back, but you couldn't find him." It was obsessive and wild, but not about sex with Lawanda: Galt was crazy. I read it again, seeing all Daddy couldn't control. Even the language—it skidded and turned and flipped—a car gone off at the curve. But this boy was in there with him. Who was he? I flipped to another page.

Always there beyond what Lawanda would want.
Before she came the buses were enough: books lined up in

182

*rows like goddamned soldiers. Some with spinal wear, not
a one shot up. Maps on the ceiling like the skin stretched
for lamp shades. Soft light through slaughter.*

*You send a man to kill in the name of family, country.
And then he sees that no matter who you shoot, it's the
same stuff flies out. It's one death, one life, I'm telling
you. So Lawanda here the first time was a return. Didn't
know enough to be scared, thought I was human.*

*Didn't know I could see her sex, her bones. Words
dancing in her mouth. Died before she was born. By my
hand somebody tied the strings to. Five-star God general.*

*A shriek in the sky, dirt explodes, and she's thrown back
into the water. And I can holler myself inside out for help
but help's crushed in a shell hole, help's oozing in a tank.
So she goes to school. Out of this bus and dying every
morning, dark streaks of ditch water in her hair.*

That's when I started shaking—in hard spasms, spilling
the coffee, rattling the notebook in my hand. I couldn't cry
here, but my throat felt swelled to splitting. Then it closed
and I made this gasping sound and I was lost in a long wave
of weeping. It's like I had struck the rock of pain, and
Daddy's, Lawanda's, mine all gushed up.

He couldn't love us because he'd killed us. Or would kill
us. So he drove us off to save us. To be alone in those buses,
in that ditch. Until Lawanda—oh God, when he finds out
about Lawanda . . . I've got to go tell him, not let Galt—

I fumbled for my purse and keys and realized two people
were standing by my table, a boy who'd been mopping and
the gray-haired woman who'd sold me the coffee.

"You okay, honey?" she asked.

I nodded. I couldn't find my voice but made motions at
the door to indicate that I was leaving. The boy looked at
his arms and legs, then moved away slowly, as if he'd just
been released from a spell.

The woman sat down in the hard chair opposite me. "It's late to be out," she said. "You sure you got somewhere to go?"

"Yes." And I was sure.

When I got in the car, I sat and breathed a minute before leaving the parking lot. The car smelled like home to me—chilled flowers from deliveries I'd made, incense from my apartment. It was comforting. Somewhere I'd had a life before this, a life to go back to.

But now I had to go back to jail. I started the motor and pulled onto the road, turning right to downtown Cardin. What I wanted to do was head for the hospital and find out how Lawanda was, but I was too frantic about Daddy. Maybe I'd even take him with me to the hospital. He belonged there as much as anybody. He sure didn't belong in jail.

"You're awful antsy," Galt said when he answered the buzzer. He was wearing gray pajamas and a robe like pillow ticking.

"It's not a night for sleeping," I told him.

"Yeah, I noticed that," he said. "What you want now?"

"Did you tell Daddy about the fire?" I asked, following him down the hall to his office.

"Shoot, no," he replied. "Let sleeping dogs lie. Or lying dogs sleep," he added, pleased with himself.

He flipped the fluorescent light on and I felt a springing in my brain, like I was not seeing, never had seen, but was getting ready for vision.

"Have a seat," he said, gesturing to the wooden chair I'd occupied just a while ago. He sat behind the desk.

"You read that thing I gave you?" he asked. His face was flushed, his gray eyes wary.

"Yes. The part you marked and a few other passages."

"And?" He leaned forward.

His question made me see the answer. "There's not a thing

in there but suffering, *private* suffering you had no right to lay eyes on. If there's a crime here, Mr. Galt"—I stood up and he wheeled his chair backward—"it's yours: invasion of privacy and unlawful detainment. And look at the ruin that's come out of it!"

He stood too. "You can't blame me—"

"Well, I do, but that's not important right now. I need to talk to my father, and I may need to take him with me."

"You're welcome to the son of a bitch," he said, and pulled a chain on his belt that drew a fist of keys from his pocket.

• • •

I could hear Daddy's snoring all the way down the hall. "Sawing logs," he used to call it. When I saw him through the bars, curled tight under a thin beige blanket, I thought, Why wake him up to this? Why take away these last hours of not knowing? But I'd come this far.

Galt switched on the light. The cell seemed even worse than before: the metal cot, suspended by chains from the wall, the steel toilet, the one rusty chair.

"Hey, Amos!" Galt called out. "You got a visitor." He unlocked the door and swung it open. "Hate to interrupt your shut-eye, but she's all fired up about something." He winked at me. I wanted to smash his face. He walked over and shook Daddy by the shoulder. "Your spitting image!" he said.

Daddy rolled over, propped himself up on one elbow, and looked at me without recognition.

"Holler when you're ready," Galt ordered, and left.

I took the chair. "Wake up, Amos," I said. "It's me, Nancy Catherine."

"You a dream?" he asked.

"No, but you're going to wish I was."

He sat all the way up. He had on somebody's worn-out

jogging suit, black with red and yellow diagonal patches. It was too little, and his hairy wrists and ankles showed.

"Something's happened to Nora," he said, like this was bad news he'd been expecting.

"No, Mother's all right. She'd . . . she'd be pleased that you thought of her—"

"I mate for life," he said. "Come on, now. State your business."

"Howard Ingle set your buses on fire and Lawanda tried to stop him."

"He done what?" Daddy rose to his feet.

I stood up, too, and took his hand. He wasn't even looking at me, didn't seem to feel my touch.

"He took a gas can, poured out a trail—"

All of a sudden, he came into focus, dropped my hand, grabbed my arms. "Did he burn them?" He shook me hard. "Are they gone?"

"Yes, yes. Stop it. There's more."

He froze. With his beard and white hair grown longer, unkempt in jail, he looked like a prophet. Only I was the one bringing word. But then he said it, low, strangled: "Lawanda!"

I nodded.

"No!" he bellowed. And he swung the chair up in one arc and smashed it against the bed. He did it again and again, till the metal legs bent. "Not Lawanda!" He ripped the blanket in half and was trying to tear the bed from the wall when suddenly he dropped, kneeling, onto it and rocked, banging his head against the cinder block. I could feel Galt staring through the bars. I grabbed Daddy's shoulders, but I couldn't stop him. I put my arms around his neck.

"She's alive," I said. "She needs you!"

He whirled around, slinging me backward. Blood cracked his forehead.

"*Needs* me?" he said sweetly. Then his voice rose. "To

strike another match, beat another woman, drown another boy?"

I grabbed him again and held on, my face against his chest. Big as I am, he's a lot bigger, and I breathed beneath the jail stink a smell I knew, his skin, the chest I used to lean against in rare times when he had me on his lap. And for the first time, I wasn't scared of him. For the first time, his misery was greater than my fear. At this release, he started to cry—just a whimper at first, but then great sobs that sounded like they broke something getting out.

"It's not your fault," I told him. "Not Lawanda. I read your journal. I know you never hurt her. And Canaan, the war—that's everybody's fault. What happened to us. You can't bear it all."

I was shaking now and we held on to each other. Finally I said, "I need to go to the hospital. You want to come?"

He drew back and saw Galt at the door.

"Clear out anytime," the jailer said. "You folks are causing a disturbance. And you'll have to pay for that chair and the blanket, Amos. That's government property."

"He has no house!" I hissed, and Galt walked away. He came back with a grocery bag of belongings they'd confiscated when Daddy was brought in. There was little in the cell to add to it. So we left, light-handed, heavyhearted. Father and daughter.

MAMAW: They wouldn't let us stay with Lawanda. Had to see how bad off she was, they said, and get her evened out. They steered her into a holding room and sent me out a-shaking. June, who until that night had always sneaked off to smoke, was puffing the waiting room full.

"I don't know which direction to cry in," she said as a few tears squoze down her face. June never was a crier. If she did get tearful as a youngun, she ran the whole time so you couldn't watch the tears. I didn't expect her to break down yet.

We was quiet. I was breathing a prayer when June's pastor showed up. Hardly older than Lawanda, he had put on a hard-times face. He said we must turn to the Lord in our hour of need. Where did he think we'd been facing? He said God wouldn't put on us more than we could bear.

"She won't," I told him, "but we do."

"Pardon?"

"This ain't the Lord's doing," I said. "This is a mess of sin we cooked up."

He scooted deeper into his seat.

"Mother Jesus"—breathe in. "Heal Lawanda"—breathe out. I was about to find the rhythm when the doctor came in, tall and puny, sweet-faced.

"You're the Ingle family?" he asked.

We all stood up. June grabbed my hand.

"I'm Dr. Graboe. And please, sit down," he said, bending himself into one of the shoehorns they got for chairs.

"She's going to make it, isn't she?" June asked, leaning forward, her grip on me tight as a claw.

"I wish I could tell you that for sure," the doctor said.

"God knows," the preacher put in.

"Looking at the percentage and degree of her burns, it could go either way."

"What does that mean?" June asked him.

He sat poker-straight. "We predict recovery on the basis of how much of the body is burned and how deeply. Anything more than twenty percent we classify as critical. Closer to sixty percent and some of it third-degree, then—"

"Them's Lawanda's figures?" I had to know.

He nodded. Then said, "Roughly. The depth of burns isn't always evident at the outset."

"How about Howard?" This was June.

"Both arms are significantly burned," Dr. Graboe told us, "but he's not in real danger. Depending on the scarring, he could have limited mobility on the left side. If that's the case, we'll do what we can to relieve it."

"Lawanda's face?" June asked, her own gone white and bony with pain.

The doctor slumped a little, looked at his hands. "You have to understand, it was the gasoline *fumes* that ignited. They were disbursed in the air. And the patient had no clothing to protect her face."

June moaned. Dr. Graboe reached out like he was going to pat her shoulder, but he didn't. "Mrs. Ingle, right now our concern is keeping your daughter alive. With so much skin gone, it's very hard to keep enough fluid in her body. Blood pressure drops. . . ." He cleared his throat. "To survive, she's going to need skin grafts as soon as she can take them. But before that, she's going to need care we can't give her here."

"Where are you taking her?" I asked.

"To the UK Medical Center in Lexington. The helicopter is on its way now."

"Helicopter?" June sounded about five years old.

"Her condition's too critical for a three-hour ambulance ride."

"She's never been on a plane," June said. "She just took her first bus trip last week."

"Can we go with her?' I asked him.

Dr. Graboe flipped through papers on his clipboard, like the answer was there.

"Not *in* the helicopter," he said. "There's room only for medical staff. And they'll be working. But we'll give you directions to the hospital, and by the time you get there, she'll be settled and you can see her."

My lips was shaking. "We need to see her before she goes," I said.

"You can do that," he said. "But only for a minute, and one at a time. Mrs. Ingle, would you—"

June about ran over him getting to the door.

JUNE: The nurse treated me like a patient or someone as old as Mommy. Had her hand under my elbow, a coo in her voice. Didn't know I don't faint. Walked me back through the blue door, told me there would be machines, tubes. She didn't know I'd been with my girl when they started all that.

The nurse said I had to wash and "suit up." She took me in a room like a trailer kitchen. I scrubbed up to my elbows, put on a gown, paper hair net, paper shoes. Then rubber gloves, like I was about to clean the oven.

"But I just saw her and I didn't have any of this!" I said. "I put my bare hand on her head."

"Well, it'll be a long day before you do that again," she told me. "Your daughter's in a sterile field now—at least as much as we can make it. Put on this mask, too." She held it out to me. "After fluid loss, infection's the greatest threat."

I did as she said, dressed up like I was going to rob bees. For Lawanda, I had to hold myself together. For Howard. I put one foot in front of the other like I was going across the kitchen. I got to her room. I got to the bed. What kind of crib had they put my baby in? High and fenced, tilted. I looked at the machines, lights, heard the whirs, whooshes. I looked at my hands. One had a red shiny spot on the back where hot grease had splashed. I remembered how fierce it

191

hurt and how it blistered. All that pain from just a skimp of flesh. "Oh, Lawanda!" I said. My womb clenched tight, as if it could take her back.

I never saw so many bandages in my life. She looked like a mummy, with just her eyes showing, and a sprig of hair.

"You cut her hair!" I said.

"What was left, yes," she said.

"Last night when she ran out the back door, she had it tied back, and it was flying out behind her, all crinkly, and I thought, That Lawanda, she's like the wind, and I was just thankful to God or Whoever that she blew through my house. And—"

"Mrs. Ingle . . ." The nurse had her arm around my back by then, heavy like a snake, a fire hose. "We've got to keep working here to get your daughter ready to move. Don't you want to tell her something?"

"Can she hear me?"

Lawanda's eyes shot open. They latched onto me like her mouth used to grab my nipple.

"I'm right here, honey," I told her. "See? They've got you wrapped up so I can't touch you. They've got me in this outfit—" Don't cry, June, don't cry, I said to myself. Don't let it out now. I took a deep breath. I wanted to give Lawanda my body, my whole skin, but all I had was words.

"Why, you're snug as a bug, Lawanda, like Mommy wrapped you after your first bath. You were a big bundle then, too. Couldn't walk or talk, couldn't feed yourself. We took care of you. There's people can do that now, honey, where they're taking you. It's just Lexington. We'll come too. Don't you worry. Your mamaw's got her prayers going. Nancy Catherine's gone to tell Garland. And your daddy—"

"Daddy?" Lawanda's voice was thin and high, squeaky.

I looked for the nurse. There was a different one across the bed.

"It's a burn voice," she said, looking quick at me and away. "It comes from trauma to the vocal cords and lungs."

192

"Trauma?"

"Smoke. Chemicals," she told me, stringing up another fluid bag.

"Daddy?" Lawanda asked again.

"He's in the hospital, too," I said, "but not hurt too bad." Not by fire, I thought.

Lawanda's eyes closed.

All I could do was pat the air around her, just pat it and think hard, Good girl. Good girl. Then the nurse latched onto my arm and pulled me away.

MAMAW: June came back looking like a scarecrow with half the stuffing gone. *You do something*, her eyes said.

She told the nurse, "Take Mommy back now. I'll go see Howard."

So a nurse led me one way and pointed June in another.

I had to wash and get all covered up, then she took me to Lawanda.

Swaddling clothes, was what I thought when I saw her. She was all bound up. And there was tubes stuck in her everywhere. Another nurse and a boy stood by her, checking machines, writing stuff down.

"We've got to get ready to roll," the nurse said. "Be quick."

"Lawanda, it's Mamaw. Are you hurting bad?" She didn't say anything and her face didn't change. "I know you can hear me, honey, somewhere in your heart. You're fixing to fly in a helicopter! Mother Jesus is coming like a big bird to pick you up, to take you where they got what you need."

I heard a clattering behind me and another boy wheeled in more doctor stuff.

"Here's your setup for the cath," the boy said to the nurse.

"I'm afraid you'll have to leave," she told me.

194

MAMAW

I leaned over and whispered in Lawanda's ear, "You know what Job said, deep in his troubles?

> "I know that my Redeemer lives
> and that at last he will stand upon the earth;
> and after my skin has been thus destroyed
> then in my flesh I shall see God.

This is awful, what you're going through, but Mother Jesus is with you, Lawanda, tied up in the same pain—"

"Time's up," the nurse said.

"And I love you, honey. I can't touch you with feathers, but I'm brooding on you. I'll be there to see you go and be right behind you all the way to Lexington."

The boy took hold of my arm.

"This way, grandma," he said, steering me out like I was blind or half-witted, one.

NANCY CATHERINE: When the adrenaline faded, it took my self-assurance with it. I shook like a tambourine as I walked Daddy to the car. How did I get into this? Wasn't it just last night I'd pulled up at this jail, determined not to let my father near me? And now I'd sprung him, more or less as my responsibility. Me, who could barely meet my flower charges month to month. I had to be nuts. It was the mountain air, or the coal dust, or the water. . . . But I knew it wasn't. It was something deep, deeper than coal.

"Good air," he said as I unlocked the passenger-side door. "In jail, you think the whole world stinks."

I took a deep breath.

Once we were in the car, I asked, "Have you ever looked into VA benefits?"

"What do you think I live on?"

"So you get a check every month?"

He nodded. I pulled out into the dark, narrow street. Drove past the drugstore, the hardware store, the florist. Very clumsy window display—I'd noticed it before.

"That's good," I went on. "Since your need for support is already established, maybe they'll be quick to see that now you need housing, too."

"What are you contemplating?"

I was contemplating how to work the one-way streets to get out of town.

"A trailer," I said.

"Two," he fired back. "I'd have to have two."

I almost laughed. "At this point, one would do you a lot of good."

He didn't respond. In a few minutes, I reached the bypass and we left the little town behind. Ahead, the black road gleamed. On either side, lights dotted the hills like stars.

"She gonna live?" he asked.

"I don't know. To tell you the truth, I kind of dropped her off and ran."

"What did she look like? What did they say?" There was anger in his voice.

"All they say in an emergency room is, 'Wait.' She looked awful. They took her away. They took Howard. Said they would come back and talk to me, but they didn't. I called her mother, picked her up, and then I came after you."

We rounded a curve and the lights of the hospital loomed. Daddy put his head down, his hand over his face. It was so strange, him sitting there, him being there physically in a dirty jacket—big-shouldered, big-chested. Not the threat of him, not his absence. I touched his sleeve. He looked over.

"Lawanda would like me hitting all the high spots," he said. "Jail, the hospital . . ."

I turned in at the divided drive. Except for the staff section, the parking lot was deserted. I pulled into a spot just off the emergency circle.

"This is it," I said, shutting off the car, setting the brake. Daddy was very still.

Then all at once, he slammed his fist on the dashboard. "Goddamn Howard Ingle!" he said. "Burn his own baby!"

"You know he never meant to."

His voice got tough. "Oh, yeah," he said. "He meant to

burn me out. His daughter's just what they call collateral damage."

My throat tightened.

He went on. "What you hit besides the target."

"Is that what happened to us?" I asked him.

He shouldered his way out of the car, stood up, and spat on the asphalt. "Come on," he said.

I didn't budge. "Is it?" I asked again, looking up. He walked off.

I scrambled after him, slamming the door. Furious, I grabbed hold of his arm to turn him around, but he was already turning. I lost my balance and would have hit the sidewalk, but he caught me.

"Yeah, N.C.," he said. "You could call it that."

GARLAND: She could call it whatever she wanted; it was Lawanda I was thinking about, not baby Nancy Catherine. But she got all blue-faced anyway, had to blow her nose before we got through the second set of doors.

"Don't run out of tears too early in the night," I told her.

With no warning, she took my arm and started shushing me, saying, "The ER is down this hall." I removed her hand.

"Back off, woman," I warned. "I ain't living in pajamas yet."

She gave this short sigh so much like her mother I could feel Nora beside me. Gave me gooseflesh.

"I tell you, I got to talk to Howard Ingle."

N.C. shrugged. It ain't polite for her to look so much like me and then act like her mother. She pushed me through a door into a waiting room. Slumped figures. Mamaw big as life.

She stood up as we walked over, held out her hand to me.

"A free man," she said when I took it.

I whistled through my teeth. The skinny woman I took to be Lawanda's mommy looked scared. Mamaw hugged Nancy Catherine.

"I'm Amos Garland," I said to Howard Ingle's wife. "I'm

199

sorry about . . . all of this. Is Lawanda going to live?"

"They can't tell yet. But they're moving her to Lexington."

"In a helicopter," Mamaw added. And then: "This is June."

We nodded at each other.

"Who's going with her?" N.C. wanted to know.

"Nobody!" June's face clenched like she would cry. "She has to go all by herself."

"She won't know—" Nancy Catherine began.

"Yes, she will," June cut in. "She's talked to me. She knows what's going on."

"That's good," Mamaw said. "Then she knows I said we'd meet her there."

"You going?" I asked June. Then her face wadded up and she really did cry.

"I want to go, but I'm afraid to leave Howard. He feels so bad. . . ."

"I got something to tell him," I said.

"He doesn't need more blame," she told me. "He's sick with it."

"Amos is the person Howard has to face," Mamaw said. "Besides Lawanda. Have a seat," she said to me. "You can't see him till morning anyhow. June just tried and he's asleep."

"Will they tell us when Lawanda goes?" N.C. asked.

"They got to," Mamaw said. "She's ours."

They all settled in. I couldn't do it. The waiting room was small and I'd just got out of jail.

"I'm going for a walk," I told N.C. "You hold down the fort."

I watched her start to say some caretaking thing, but she was smart—she didn't. I got out fast.

The night air was wet and cold. Had that moss-on-rocks smell that mountains make. Felt good to my skin. I tried not to think about Lawanda's. I tried to think about getting a government trailer with heat, maybe water. But I kept seeing her face rise like the sun over my ridge, kept hearing her brand-new voice holler my name.

I don't know how many times I hiked around the hospital before I heard the chopper coming in. The way sound bounces off these hills, it could have been a squadron instead of just a single on loan from the National Guard. I watched it land, then made my way to the pad, which was on the ground, not the roof.

The medics were already out when I got there, hair and clothes blown by the rotor wake. They headed for the hospital. The door opened before they reached it and a tall skinny man began rolling Lawanda out. A herd of people was around and behind her, like dogs following the gut wagon. I saw N.C. coming toward me.

They slid a stretcher from the helicopter, moved Lawanda onto it, with all her tubes and bags. I couldn't see much, didn't want to—I've seen enough, buddy. I know what fire does. I thought, Even if she lives through this, that girl is gone.

And then I heard Lawanda far away, back in First Bus, say, "I think you're beautiful," to me, all warped and grizzled. By God, that was forgiveness. I went right over to her.

She struggled to move, bandaged and hooked up like she was, and her eyes were looking everywhere. "Lawanda!" I said, and she focused on me. "Thank you!"

Then the crew lifted her, tilting the head of the stretcher up to get it into the helicopter. Suddenly Mamaw and June were there too.

"I've got to stay with your daddy now, Lawanda, but I'll come in a day or two," June said.

"We've got to fly!" the nurse declared. "Everybody back!"

"Mother Jesus is riding with you," Mamaw hollered, "and I'll be driving underneath."

Then the stretcher and crew were in, the doors shut, and a doctor waved us back into the hospital. We watched through the windows as the rotors gained speed and carried Lawanda away.

LAWANDA: I think I'd be all right if I
could just get free of all this, if I could just get up and move
around. But I'm tied and tethered—there's even something
going into my chest—and I'm shut in this machine who
knows where in the sky. I want down! I want out! It's so
loud, they couldn't hear me if they were listening. Which
they're not. Too busy saving me to find out how I am.

Mamaw said Mother Jesus was sending a big bird to take
me—yeah, like an eagle takes a mouse.

My throat hurts. Most of my body feels somewhere else,
but my throat has a knife in it and it's turning, like you core
an apple.

He said, "Thank you!" For what?

As long as I'm up here, I'd like to see out, but I can't
find any windows. It kind of bumps along. What happens
if I throw up?

The nurse holds a pan. She says my pressure is better and
they can give me something that might make me sleep. "Just
a drop or two," she says, and squirts it into a tube. Her
name tag says Barbara.

• • •

"Barbara," I call in a new place, the ceiling rushing above
me. She doesn't appear. Bright—maybe it's morning now.

203

"This is the Burn Unit," somebody says. "You've got your own bed waiting."

That's a first. I've always shared with Dessie. Jeff, too, when he was just out of the crib. Dad said Noonie and Ray would roll on him.

Noonie's gone now. I'm gone. Jeff sleeps with Ray. Dessie's got her own bed.

A nurse says her name is Treasure. Maybe my name is Lost Wealth. Like Lawanda, you know? She smiles, I think. Her mouth's behind a mask, but her eyes are hopping. All the workers wear masks, cover their hair, wear gloves. Great place for a robbery.

A doctor comes up—Dr. Hostage. That can't be right. He says they have to evaluate and transfer and change dressings and they might as well do this all at once. I nod. I don't know what I'm in for.

A terrible smell, for one thing, as soon as the dressings are opened—sick-sweet. At first I don't know where it's coming from. Rotten chicken, I think. Bury it. Freeze it. Then I understand: Oh God, it's me! Then comes the first slash of pain. The nurses have to pull off what's stuck, and when that's done, they have to wash and scrub.

"Go ahead and scream," Treasure says, and I would if my throat would. I make noises more like a stepped-on cat. Treasure says she's sorry they can't put me in the whirlpool. I picture spinning. "In a few days," she says. I have to stay here for days?

It's torture till they've poured on all their medicines and bound me up again. They put me in a big bed with fences. Pain quits shouting and just sings. I ask if Mamaw's come yet.

"Mamaw?" they say, eyebrows rising up to their hair nets.

I try something else. "Then could I have some soup beans?" I ask.

"These people," Treasure says, and sighs. "These people from the mountains."

GARLAND: As we walked back to the waiting room, I felt like I still had to see Howard Ingle, but now my message was different. I didn't want to rant. Could I say, "She's forgiven me, she'll forgive you too"? That wouldn't make sense to him. Could I say I did the same thing to my daughter, only it started half a world away? Collateral damage? Could I say Canaan died, but Lawanda might not? No, I couldn't tell all that. It would mean explaining my whole life. Still, I had to talk to him. I said this to the family when we all got seated.

Mamaw agreed. June wasn't sure. I told her I wasn't carrying blame. Nancy Catherine raised her eyebrows. "It's different since I saw Lawanda," I said. June covered her face with her hands.

Mamaw patted her shoulder. "You go first," she said to June. "Tell Howard where Lawanda's gone. You'll feel better when that's done."

June took her hands down. She looked like the hind end of bad luck. "It's getting light," she said. "He'll be waking up." And she left.

She wasn't gone long, and she came back looser around the edges.

"He says he cried so hard, he threw up," she told us. "So they gave him a knockout shot. That's why he was asleep when I went before."

This fact seemed to make her feel better.

"You told him Amos was coming?" Mamaw asked.

June nodded.

"Better get it over with," Nancy Catherine said.

"Nothing gets over with," I told her. "That's what I'm going to say."

. . .

I took the elevator to the third floor, and a nurse walked me down to Howard's room, warning all the way, "Don't upset him," like he had no cause to be upset. "Let him enjoy his breakfast," she said when we passed the cart with all the trays. I held my tongue.

At room 307, the nurse pushed the door open. Green and skin tan walls, like the whole place.

"Mr. Ingle, Mr. Garland's here to see you," she announced, then made mouth motions to me: Five minutes.

I went in. Howard Ingle is a small man, and now he looked drawn up like he'd had a stroke. His arms were held out from his sides, thick with dressings. His face was turned to the window.

"You know who I am," I said, and he looked at me. He nodded. "I got to tell you something. I done what you done."

Howard stared at me, face white, eyes sunk in.

"I set a fire once, away across the ocean. The army gave me the gas can, the matches. All that water between here and there and still it burnt my family."

"That was war," Howard Ingle said.

"What do you call this?" I asked him.

He shut his eyes.

"I wanted to protect the boys they gave me. I thought I could, too, like I'd watched over my high school kids back home. But these boys were *killing* people, you see. That was their job. I told them to do it. That was the purpose of our travels, our outfits. So the killing came back to us. Same as if a kid tries to throw a cherry bomb out a closed window. Comes back and blows up in his face. And the window's always closed, buddy. It may be far away, so it'll take years for the force to get back. But it'll come . . . it'll come. You were right at the window, Howard Ingle. You didn't have to wait."

He couldn't wipe the tears from his face with his arms bandaged. I swiped at them with a Kleenex.

"What are you telling me?" he asked.

"That what you did to me, you did to yourself. And that I've done it too."

Howard Ingle flinched, as if I'd hit him. "But it's *Lawanda*—" he started out, his voice rising.

"Lawanda flat-out believed I was human," I told him. "She forgave me. She'll do the same for you."

"But I burned your buses," he said.

"And I shelled towns," I gave back. "Scalded my kids' dreams. You think I could send you to jail?"

"I was wrong about you," he said.

And I answered, "So was I."

HOWARD: It wasn't that easy, by God.
Nobody knows what Lawanda went through. I come the closest because I did have burns, but they were nothing like Lawanda's. And the scars don't matter on me, long as my hands work, long as my arms can lift and bend. But Lawanda's a *girl*, headed toward being a woman. And she used to be pretty as a clear sky, not that she paid much heed to it. Now she has to. Everybody does.

She was four months in the hospital. Four months a hundred and fifty miles from home. June and Mamaw taking turns staying with her. Me visiting sometimes. Nancy Catherine taking Garland the first time, on her way home to Louisville. He rode back with Mamaw and took my job till I got better. Had to get a driver's license to do it. Garland hadn't driven since the war. And he was no great hand as a route man. Kept passing roads he recognized, then turning back for a little tour.

He kept sober, though, at least on the job. Curtis Ballard fixed him a cot in the boiler room. Got him a hot plate. There's a bathroom at the cleaners. Much better than a bus. Now he's back on the ridge in a HUD trailer. And he has a truck, but I'll get to that.

Lawanda's a different person is all I can say. She says she's not.

"A part of me that was way back in there has just moved forward," she told me. But that's the kind of thing she never would have said.

She's been through so much. The stuff they do to you—bathing and scraping, robbing one crop of skin to plant another, having her face patched together like a roof. Like when you can't afford to strip the whole thing and start over. Just bring hot tar and shingles and do what you can.

Oh, Lawanda!

June'll never be the same either. Let's just say it. We're every one scarred. Ray ran off. Noonie found him. He was headed north. Whenever he ran out of money, he'd just sell blood.

"Think about it," Garland said. "You could ride your own red river all the way to Canada."

Lawanda said it's not red, it's plasma.

Whatever color it is, thank the Lord he couldn't do it. Thank the Lord he's back on the school bus, riding to school. Still almost as mad at me as I am. We just abide each other.

Dessie didn't leave us by running away. She just acts like we're not related. She talks about circumstance, like that's all this is. I didn't know she knew a word that big. And Jeff, my least one, he's afraid of me. I can tell when I swoop him up. All his bones lock. I thought maybe it was because of the scars on my arms, but he went straight up to Lawanda. Sat by her side, reached up to touch her face. "Does it hurt?" he asked. She shook her head and smiled and left the room.

Then there's June. She's the one's come forward, it seems to me. She wants everything firsthand now, said she's through being treated "like the dummy and the discard." You should have seen her with Lawanda's doctors. She looked things up in books and then asked them questions just like they was people. She'd back them up in a corner, not leave a thing to Mamaw or me. And when I was back at work and her pa began to wander, she went straight to

Garland. Hired him to help with the farm and to stay with John when Mamaw was in Lexington. Got John's old truck towed and fixed. That's how Garland got wheels. If you'd told me a year ago we'd look to that old man for help, I'd of said you was crazy. But the world has turned.

Anyway, to my knowledge, Garland's been reliable. Oh, he and Nancy Catherine got into it once when she was here. She says he threw things. Doesn't surprise me. I'll bet she did too. They're that alike. The surprise is that they made up. A big wad of thorns and sometimes roses.

Lawanda would say that. She would. It's probably the kind of thing she writes in her notebook. She's taken to keeping notebooks, just like Garland. Now I'd think if anything would put you off writing, all this would, but that's not the way of it.

It may be because Lawanda read so much in the hospital. Listened to taped books before she could hold one in her hand. And she got real deep into music. Singing. She had to sing as part of her treatment, to build her voice back. Garland would take his harmonica; Nancy Catherine brought a friend with a guitar. Now Lawanda sings all the time. Makes up songs too. Writes those in the notebook.

She's solid, Lawanda is. Still planning to go to college. She'll do it too. This summer, she's making up the math she missed in the hospital. Garland helped her stay caught up on the rest.

And I'm looking around me real hard all the time and trying to see what life is like, trying not to label it. Even my life. That's the hardest. I can feel so bad, so sick at myself, like I ought to crawl off in the woods and die. But that would just mean more pain for June, and no money. Mamaw said, "If Lawanda can live, you can too."

So there you have it.

LAWANDA: Now that Garland's living in the world, I can't just hike up Cade's Hill anytime and expect him to be there. The truth is, I can't hike. I can walk very slowly up the access road HUD cut to put in the trailer. But I call first. Garland protested about getting a phone, but Mom said if he was working for her, he'd have to. Isn't that weird?

Anyway, the other day I called and he said to come on up. Even offered to come and get me. But I explained I'd get my therapy out of the way by walking, and if it wore me out, he could bring me home.

It's strange going up there. So strange, so familiar. The ground is scarred, the buses gone, and Garland lives in a place with a regular door! It's got *carpet*, a couch, a kitchen with running water: weird. Sometimes it seems fake, like somebody put a new background behind Garland's life the way they do in movies. But it's real as a helicopter.

And it's full of books. More books than anything, even in the kitchen cabinets. "Reference section," Garland says. One bedroom has the maps. New maps, of course. Including a star map and one of the United States that shows where his kids are. Garland's come back from the war.

This day, Tuesday, he welcomed me in, gave me orange juice, asked how I was doing.

211

"Algebra is not all that exciting, but I'm getting it done."

"I thought you liked math," he said.

"I do. But I liked it better when I thought things only had one answer."

"Makes sense to me."

That made me smile. It's so good to be with someone you make sense to.

I was thinking about this when he said, "Can I read you something?"

Now there's a difference. Before the fire, he would have said, "Listen to this." I was the kid. He was the grown-up. Now we're both veterans.

"Sure," I said. "Read away."

He dug in a stack of papers and notebooks on the kitchen counter. "Ah," he said. "Here it is." He held up a magazine. "Found this in Lexington. Little bitty article. What they call a filler. Listen:

> "A summer or so after the end of the Second World War, Londoners noticed strange plants growing in the bomb craters, rare flowers flourishing. Botanists were called in and, through intense study, they made this discovery: though native to London, the plants had not grown there since 1666. The Great Fire had burned them off, buried their seed under ash and rubble. Nearly three hundred years later, the blaze and force of bombs resurrected them."

He looked up at me. I just stared. I didn't like what he read.

"Don't you get it?" he asked.

"Maybe." I was mad, but I tried to let it go. "What's the Great Fire?"

"Somebody left the stove on and accidentally torched the city. It was London's worst disaster until the bombs."

"Okay," I said, teeth clenched.

"But look here, don't you—"

"No. I don't." I closed my eyes to block him out but he went on.

"It's like . . ."

"Just stop it!" I ordered, standing up. Slowly. Only my mind was fast now. Only my tongue. "I get it, all right. How neat. They had fire, then bombs. But we got the bombs first." I started pacing around his tiny space. "And when the fire came, it just burned the mange off the mountain. And the skin off me. Or am I supposed to be the flower, only charred?"

"Lawanda—" Garland was on his feet now too, his hands lifted like this was a holdup.

"Or am I the seed blasted free?" My voice twisted. "Tell me, Poetry Man. In this great epic, where do I wind up, scarred for life?"

In a kitchen, I thought, by a refrigerator, at the end of my rope. With sky out the trailer window instead of sky out the windshield of First Bus.

Garland came over to me and put his hands on my shoulders. His face looked different.

"It *is* for life, Lawanda. That's all I'm saying. Life will come out of it." And there were tears on his cheeks, Garland tears.

"Oh God," I said, and took him in my arms.